TEXAS TEMPTATION
Making a Family Series, Book One

BARBARA MCMAHON

Texas Temptation
Copyright © 2024 Barbara McMahon
All Rights Reserved

Prologue

Jordan Carhart hated spring break. It wasn't only because of the long hours, though for those two weeks every spring her shifts doubled up and days off were only a memory. She was certain half the college students from eastern schools and most of the ones in the Midwest flocked to South Beach to party hardy. They came to drink, have fun and fall in love.

It was the best of times because of the extra tips and the exuberant spirits rampant among the visitors.

It was the worst of times because of the memories that surfaced. Memories kept tucked away for most of the year. Only the lingering sadness remained when she looked into her son's eyes.

Jordan wiped the table, stacking glasses and dishes in the bin. Where was that blasted busboy? Honestly, if she were the manager of Joe's Fish Tacos, she'd fire Manuel and hire someone more reliable.

Lifting the heavy bin, she carried it into the kitchen and dumped it by the sink. The steam from the simmering pots and soup cauldrons made the restaurant's kitchen an instant steam bath. The greasy smell of frying shrimp filled the air. She glanced at the counter. None of her orders were up yet, so she escaped to the relative coolness of the restaurant proper.

Glancing around her assigned area with a practiced eye, Jordan noticed the group of giggling college girls were about to leave. She watched as they laughed among themselves and threw saucy glances at the boys that wandered into view on the spacious open-air deck. Skimpy swimsuits were the order of the day. And the coverups never did their job, revealing more than concealing.

She'd worn one such over her own bikini five years ago when—

No, she would not go there again. It'd been five years, time to move on beyond the Cinderella story that had an unhappy ending. She was older and far wiser now than she'd been then. Never again would she get caught up in the frenzy and romance of spring break. Never listen to lies wrapped in romantic overtones. Nor believe a man when he said he loved her after only two weeks.

Now she was a single mother, with a son who gave her more delight than she had a right to. Her life hadn't taken the path she'd wanted so long ago, but she wouldn't trade Caleb for all the tea in China, as her aunt Maggie used to say.

Nothing came without a price, however. She smiled at the girls when they waved on their way out, hoping they left a large tip. They'd been extravagant in ordering, then left half the food on the table. Sure enough, they'd been equally lavish in their tips.

Jordan scooped up the money and put it in her pocket. Another few dollars for Caleb's surgery fund. Her goal was to save enough to have the operation done before he started school next year. It wasn't right that a little boy should have crossed eyes. She'd done her best to shelter him from cruel insults, but she knew starting school that way would cause unmerciful teasing. She refused to accept that for her son.

But since the surgery was elective rather than lifesaving, the meager insurance coverage she had from the restaurant didn't cover the procedure. The full cost would have to be borne by her. And she was still a few thousand dollars short.

Jordan stacked the dishes from the crowded table in another bin, resigned to the fact Manuel had disappeared once again. Taking the discarded newspaper, she folded it and tucked it beneath her arm. She enjoyed reading the newspapers from all over that customers left. Once she'd had dreams of leaving South Beach and seeing Atlanta, or Washington, or even New York. But dreams of college and travel had vanished from her horizon when she'd become pregnant with Caleb.

She dumped the dishes, then served another two tables before time for her break. Reaching for the purloined newspaper, she hurried outside, away from the din and commotion. Sitting beneath a huge old palm, which offered scant shade in the heat of the day, she spread open the paper. It was the *Dallas Tribune*. For a second, her heart clutched.

She looked up, glimpsing the blue Atlantic between the souvenir shops and sidewalks crowded with randy college kids. It was as if she looked into the past. Texas. *He* had been from Texas.

Sighing softly, she picked up the paper and scanned the

various articles. She was almost finished with the front section when a small headline on the lower left caught her eye.

Cade Cullen Everett and Family Donate One Million Dollars to the Children's Last Wish Foundation.

Jordan started at the words, unable to believe her eyes.

Cade Cullen Everett.

Five years vanished immediately, and she was once again the young girl who had been swept away by the big brash Texan who had charmed her socks off, overcome her innate inhibitions and seduced her into bed.

Two weeks of heaven. The glamour of it, the rush of excitement, the heady delight, the spellbinding glory of those days filled her mind. Her heart raced in memory. She had enjoyed luxurious wining and dining. Told over and over, she was the prettiest thing he'd ever seen. She could almost hear the echo of that sexy Texas drawl.

Then—he'd vanished without a word. Spring break had ended, and he'd returned to Texas.

Jordan never heard from him again.

She hadn't known where to contact him. She'd poured over telephone books and searched the Internet, trying to locate any and every Everett to contact and ask if they knew Cade Cullen, especially after she had discovered she was pregnant. The man should know he was to become a father.

To no avail. No one she talked to claimed to know him. It was as if he vanished from the face of the earth.

Until now.

Quickly she read the article. A ranch was mentioned in Tumbleweed, Texas. She remembered his wild and outlandish stories of the family ranch. Most she'd taken with a grain of salt, but the basis must have been true, she'd thought. No wonder she'd never found him in the city phone books. He lived in a town she'd never heard of—fifty miles west of Fort Worth.

The gist of the article centered on the magnificent grant he and his family provided. One million dollars.

Anger simmered. His disappearance had cheated Caleb of knowing his father. And from the article, he had the means to give Caleb proper care from the beginning. She'd been saving for more than four years for the operation that would enable Caleb's eyes to track properly. Scraping together every dime she could manage, doing without so they could add to the surgery fund.

She only needed two thousand dollars more and her son would have surgery, which would make eyes track like everyone else.

A man who could donate one million dollars to a charity could certainly pony up a mere two thousand dollars for his own son's operation.

She reread the article. He donated the money in memory of his wife and daughter.

So he'd gone back home and married some Texas girl.

Jordan had long ago acknowledged the emotions she'd felt for Cade Cullen Everett had been one-sided. No man, no matter how much he professed to love her, would have stayed away and never contacted her. He knew where she lived. He could have called or written or come back to South Beach if she'd meant anything to him.

The feelings she'd had for him had died long ago.

But Caleb was his son. And by Jove, she was going to let the man know about the boy. Every child deserved a father. Maybe Caleb's father could pay his fair share of the needed operation.

And if he gave her any grief, wouldn't the Dallas paper love to hear how the generous man and his family refused to help his own son?

Rising, Jordan strode into the café, eager for her shift to end. As soon as she finished, she was calling Cade Cullen Everett. Armed with the name of the town, she was sure she could find him with no trouble at all. Wouldn't he be surprised to hear a voice from the past?

Chapter One

Jordan peered through the rain at the ornate wrought-iron gate that marked the entrance to the Circle E Ranch. She sneezed again and blew her nose. Rubbing her aching chest, she tried to take a deep breath. It hurt to breathe.

This had been the trip from hell. If the blasted man had answered any of her letters, or returned a single phone call, she wouldn't have had to drive from Florida to Texas. But he'd ignored her as completely this past month as he had over the last five years.

Not that Jordan was going to let his behavior stop her. She'd taken a week's vacation from work, pushed her ancient car to the limit and here they were in Tumbleweed, Texas, turning onto the Everett Ranch.

The car had broken down in Biloxi. And again in that raging thunderstorm outside of Beaumont. Her cold had gotten worse by the day, made even more so after standing in the pouring rain while talking to the tow truck driver.

Determined, she pushed on. She would not be ignored or blown off. If Cade Cullen Everett thought refusing to respond to her demands would make her forget them, he didn't know her.

Of course, she thought as they inched up the drive in the downpour; he *hadn't* known her—not really. A brief two-week fling was one thing. Romantic and exciting, but not of the real world.

More fool her for believing him when he told her he loved her. Hadn't her aunt warned her time after time? If she'd only listened.

Yet if she had, she wouldn't have Caleb, and she wouldn't trade him for anything. Wouldn't Cullen wish to learn he had a son?

"Are we there yet Mommy?" Caleb asked from his car seat in the back.

"Almost, honey," she responded, hoping it was true. Truth to tell, she hoped she could last long enough to challenge Cullen and get his agreement to help pay for the surgery before they had to leave to find a motel for the night. She wanted nothing more than to crawl into bed and pull the covers over her head and sleep until morning.

Florida was famous for summer afternoon thundershowers, but she was wondering if Texas had them beat. This was the third stormy day in a row.

"Will we see horses?" he asked.

"I don't know. They might be inside the barn because of the rain."

They could see plenty of cattle grazing in the fields flanking the road, but no horses.

"How about cows?" he persisted.

"Look out your window. There are more cows than you can count."

The large herd covered several acres, many of the steers standing stoically, backs lined up to the wind, placidly enduring the rain as it poured down.

The driveway was like a county road, two lanes wide, paved and straight as an arrow. How far to the house? Cresting a slight rise, Jordan had her answer.

Ahead rose a huge house, white, two stories tall, with soaring columns supporting the roof that covered a wide veranda. It looked large enough to hold a multi generation family. It reminded her of Tara—splashy, but suitable for a family who could donate one million dollars to charity.

Beyond the house were the ranch buildings, two enormous barns and an assortment of other buildings and sheds. She hadn't a clue about how ranches worked. What were all the structures for? A small brick building sat to the left of the house. It looked like an office to her, squat, with tall windows—looking like many insurance offices in Florida.

"Wow," Jordan thought, stunned at the size of the place. She slowed the car and stared. She thought Cullen's bragging had been the wild tales of a college guy on the prowl out to impress. It looked as if he hadn't exaggerated one bit.

Suddenly doubt crept in.

Was she doing the right thing? Maybe she should have left Caleb with her friend Patricia and come alone. Suddenly, a horrifying thought sprang to mind. What if Cullen wanted visiting rights?

Or even custody?

According to the article, he'd lost his wife and child in a terrible automobile accident. Maybe he'd want his son near him.

She felt a pang of sympathy for the man, even though she

remained angry at his behavior toward her. How awful to lose a wife, but more especially a child. He wouldn't want Caleb permanently, would he?

Jordan hesitated, wondering if she'd made the trip for nothing. She'd taken precious funds from their savings for this trip, but she considered it well spent if she could get Caleb's father to pay the balance of the expense. Doubts not withstanding, she couldn't turn back without seeing him, without trying to get him to pay a share, not when she was this close. And he deserved to meet his son. She hoped he'd like Caleb, but be content to leave their current living arrangement intact.

"Why aren't we driving, Mommy? I see a house. The lights are on and it's only afternoon."

"I know, sweetie. It's because of the rain."

It was shortly after noon, yet it was so dark from the storm she needed her headlights. The glow through the windows in the house gave the illusion of welcome. Slowly, she headed forward. She'd come all this way. She needed to see it through. For Caleb's sake.

Stopping near the front door, Jordan turned off the engine and reached back to unfasten Caleb's safety belt.

"Climb over the seat and let's go," she said.

Coughing for a moment, she waited while he scrambled over the seat back and stood beside her. She really felt awful. She hoped this encounter would go smoothly.

"We'll walk really fast so we don't get soaked, okay?" she said.

If she'd had an umbrella, she'd have tried to carry him and

kept them both dry, but she hadn't thought to bring one. And she felt so tired and weak she didn't think she could carry him the short distance to the veranda. Maybe she should have gotten a room in Tumbleweed first, taken a nap and then come. Too late now.

She thrust open her door and hurried them to the front of the house.

"Whee," Caleb said as he splashed in puddles between the car and the covered veranda.

Great, Jordan thought, as she tried to hurry him along. They'd both show up looking like drowned rats.

She rang the doorbell and shivered slightly in the breeze. Her shoulders and hair were damp from their mad dash. The wind cooled her quickly, blowing through her wet clothes as if she wore nothing.

The door opened. An older Hispanic woman stood in the opening, her dark hair streaked with gray, bounded at the back of her head in a tidy bun. A large apron covered her full skirted dress.

"Can I help you?" she asked.

She held a dish towel in one hand. Her expression was pleasant, but curious.

"I'm looking for Cade Cullen Everett," Jordan said.

Caleb peeked around her to look at the woman, his eyes wide.

"Señor Everett is busy. Was he expecting you?"

"No, but we've come a long way. I only need a few minutes of his time."

Jordan had come too far to be turned away. She was

prepared to wait for however long it took.

The older woman studied Jordan for a moment, then looked at Caleb, her expression softening into a smile.

"Step in out of the storm. I'll tell him you are here if you give me your name."

"Jordan Carhart."

No sooner had she said it than she began coughing again. Her chest hurt so badly. And she felt flushed. They kept the house too warm, or was it the contrast to the coldness from the storm?

"Who is it Rosita?" a male voice called.

Jordan turned and watched as a stranger strode into the entryway. He frowned when he looked at her and then spotted Caleb.

His hair was dark and cut short. His forbidding expression made him look even more intimidating than his size alone would have done. He was several inches over six feet, muscular and tanned.

For a moment she remembered the skinny college kids who strutted so arrogantly on the beach during spring break. She couldn't imagine this man ever looking like that. But he could give them all lessons on sex appeal and how to capture a woman's attention.

Despite feeling terrible because of her cold, Jordan was intrigued.

The rugged jaw told Jordan he wasn't someone to be trifled with. His tanned skin attested to hours spent in the sun. His fit body didn't come from some gym. Was he a relative of Cullen's? Too young to be his father. Was he an older brother?

She guessed he wasn't too much older than thirty.

A cough caught her. Her perusal cut short. She didn't have time to speculate. She was on a mission—as soon as she could catch her breath.

"I'm looking for Cade Cullen Everett," Jordan said firmly.

"You've found him," the man said.

She blinked. The world seemed to tilt and sway.

Caleb peeped around her leg and looked up at the man.

"Are you my daddy?" he asked.

It was the last thing Jordan heard before everything went black as she softly sank to the floor.

Cade dashed forward, barely catching her before her head hit the hardwood floor.

"Mommy?"

The little boy clung to his mother's leg as she sagged in Cade's arms.

"Mommy, what's wrong?"

His eyes wide with fear, the child clung to Jordan.

Cade shifted and lifted her.

"Your mom will be okay, son. Let me take her into the living room to lie down."

He carried her into the spacious room and placed her on the wide sofa. The little boy ran to her head and patted her shoulder.

"Mommy?" Fear laced his tone.

"She'll be okay," Cade said again, studying the unconscious woman, hoping she'd come around soon. Color stained her cheeks. Her breathing was raspy. She couldn't weigh more than a hundred pounds, which on her made her too thin.

"Should I call the doctor?" Rosita asked poised in the doorway, her face full of concern.

"Not yet. Let's see if she wakes up in a minute on her own," Cade said, studying the unconscious woman.

Just what he didn't need, a further complication to an already complicated day.

"I'll get a cool cloth," she said, heading for the back of the house.

This wasn't the best of times for unexpected visitors. Not when his long-term secretary had just informed him she was needed at home for a family emergency and would leave that afternoon. Her mother had fallen and broken her hip. There was no one else to see to the elderly woman but Penny. Still, the timing couldn't have been worse.

Not when he had a minor crisis building into a major one in Los Angeles.

Not when it was time to muster the herd and rotate cattle from the winter pasture to summer fields. He'd come home to the ranch for that event, which had already been delayed once this spring and was currently delayed because of the weather. If not for the muster, he'd still be in Dallas, or maybe even on his way to LA.

He had a dozen irons in the fire. He didn't need further complications.

"Why is Mommy asleep?" the boy asked. "She never takes naps."

"What's your name, son?" he asked. He'd never seen either of them before, but hadn't imagined the child's comment, *"Are you my daddy?"* Who were these people?

"I'm Caleb," he said. "Is Mommy going to wake up soon?"

"I expect so. Caleb who? Where are you from?"

Caleb wrinkled his brow as he looked up at Cade.

He felt a hitch when he saw the uncertainty in the child's eyes. For a heartbeat, they reminded him of Vicki's bright blue eyes. Except in this case, one definitely turned inward. He knew little about it, but shouldn't the child have had some corrective work done by this age?

Rosita hurried into the room, carrying a cool, damp cloth. She placed it on Jordan's forehead and felt her cheeks with the back of her fingers.

"She had a fever, señor."

"Who is she?"

"Her name is Jordan Carhart. She asked for you, said she came a long way to see you. Maybe we ought to call the doctor," she murmured.

The little boy looked up at him.

"Are you my daddy?" he asked again.

"No."

Cade knew that for a fact. Not only had he never seen the woman before in his life, the boy looked to be about four or five years old. And five years ago, he'd been a happily married man. Cheating on his wife had never once occurred to him. He'd loved Marissa more than life.

The familiar ache gripped him. Would he ever get over losing her? Ever get used to the gaping hole in his heart that she and Vicki once filled?

"Mommy said we were coming to meet my daddy. Where is he?"

Cade's instincts went on alert. She'd asked for him by name and told her son he was his father. What kind of scam was the woman trying to pull?

With her blond hair and gray eyes, and the boy's blue eyes, there was no way they could accuse him of being the father, not with his dark hair and eyes. DNA testing would cinch it if needed.

"Mommy," Caleb said, shaking her. "Wake up, Mommy."

Cade felt a tightening in his throat. The kid looked scared to death. He remembered Vicki when she'd been five. All bright laughter and boundless energy. Nothing had scared her.

No child should be so scared.

He squatted down beside the youngster and took one small hand in his. Memories crowded in. He remembered holding Vicki's hand when they crossed a street or went to a store. Echoes of her laughter sounded. He could still see her delight in so many everyday things.

This child looked nothing like his daughter, but just his being here reminded Cade of all he'd lost.

"Where do you live, Caleb?"

"Seventeen-thirty Atlantic Circle, South Beach," the boy said proudly. Obviously his mother made sure he knew his address.

"Florida?" Cade murmured, wondering if Vicki had known her address at that age.

"We've been driving forever, and Mommy said we'd see my daddy when we got here. We need money for my eyes.

Once I have my operation, I can be just like all the other little boys, but until then, I'm special."

Rosita threw Cade a look.

"Shall I take the boy into the back so you can talk to the mother when she wakens?" she asked practically.

"I can't leave Mommy," Caleb protested.

"Your Mommy's going to be fine," Cade said, standing. "Let her rest for a few minutes. Rosita can give you a cookie and some milk. I bet you're hungry."

Caleb seemed to consider the offer.

"I am hungry. We didn't get lunch yet. Can I have lunch?" Caleb asked.

"Sure thing. Rosita, would you?"

When the housekeeper led the little boy away, he reached for the phone. It rang directly into the office.

"Yes, boss?" Penny answered, recognizing the inter-ranch line.

"Before you leave, call Paul Nance for me. I have a young woman who fainted in the entryway. She seems to have a fever and difficulty breathing. See if he thinks we need to bring her into emergency."

"Will do."

Penny disconnected. Cade almost smiled. Nothing fazed Penny. Not a stranger collapsing in the house, or anything else that happened around the ranch. She was as invaluable here as she was in the Dallas office. What was he going to do with her gone for who knew how long?

And she didn't know how long she'd be gone. Penny had already called the local employment agency to send a temp, but Cade knew it wouldn't be easy working with a stranger.

The woman stirred. Good. If she came to, he could send her on her way, with a suggestion she stop off at the doctor's in town. One problem solved.

The phone rang just as those gray eyes opened again.

"Everett," Cade responded when he picked up.

"Cade? Heard you have someone who might need medical help," Paul's voice came across the line. He and Cade had gone to high school together. Paul had then gone to study medicine while Cade had specialized in business. Their paths didn't cross often these days, but the bond of friendship remained strong.

"I think she's coming out of it. Hold on," Cade squatted again beside the sofa, his eyes almost on a level with hers.

"Are you feeling better?" he asked.

Slowly, she blinked and stared at him.

"What happened?"

Her gaze darted around the room, confusion clear.

"Where's Caleb?"

A hint of panic sounded in her voice. She tried to sit up, but Cade put his hand on her shoulder and pressed her back against the cushions.

"He's fine, in with Rosita, having lunch. It's you we're concerned with. You fainted."

"Fainted? I never faint." She rubbed her forehead. "I don't feel too well."

Cade put the receiver back to his ear.

"She's awake and lucid. I think the crisis has passed. I'll send her in to see you. Thanks for calling back."

"No problem. Let me know if you need anything."

Cade hung up the phone and rose to his full height. At over six feet, she had a long way to look up. The confusion hadn't left her expression.

"You are not Cade Cullen Everett," she mumbled.

"I was the last time I looked. But obviously not the one you were expecting. Never knew there were two of us."

She closed her eyes, tears seeping from between the lids.

"Can I get you something?" Cade asked, wondering who Jordan Carhart was, and why she was looking for him—or rather, some man who had the same name.

She shook her head. "I'll be out of your way in a minute. Sorry for the misunderstanding. I thought—I saw an article in the Dallas paper that reported your donation to the Children's Last Wish Foundation. I thought I'd found the man I've been looking for for years. I mean, I thought you were Cade Cullen Everett. My Cade Cullen Everett. Actually, not mine, exactly. But I've been looking for him for five years. I thought I'd finally located him."

"You came a long way based on a newspaper article. Your son said you live in Florida."

"I tried writing, calling, but you never responded. I was desperate."

"Because?"

Cade sat on the chair flanking the sofa. Before Jordan could say another word, his Aunt Amelia swirled into the room, her lacy dress more suitable for a garden party than the ranch house. But he was used to it. Fancy feminine dresses were her standard attire.

He sighed. Another complication he did not need.

"Oh, nephew, I'm so pleased you knew to call on me in case of an emergency. I'm happy to help in any way I can. Is this the poor dear? Oh, she looks ill."

Jordan stared at the elderly woman, delicate in statue with soft white hair curled around her face. Her dress reminded her of southern parties and gentile living. Feminine and flighty, Jordan summed up in one thought. And a bit out of place in the room, which had a strong southwest decor.

She glanced at the rugged man, who looked pained for a split second at the arrival of the older woman. He quickly schooled his features.

Could they really be in the same family? She'd called him nephew, but he looked too large, too masculine to be connected to this ethereal woman.

"How do you feel, dear?" She fluttered over and patted Jordan's cheeks. "Oh, you are burning up. Cade," she looked at her nephew, "she's burning up. We need to give her something for the fever. Aspirin. I think aspirin would be fine. And fluids. Plenty of fluids. Clear like apple juice or water."

When Jordan began coughing, Amelia raised her handkerchief to her cover her nose and mouth, still fluttering around.

"Oh dear, that cough is terrible. Cade, we must do something about that as well. Bed rest will help. Should she have the lilac room or the rose? Lilac, I think, it's so soothing, and the rose will confuse the issue about her fever, don't you think? She's flushed enough without pink from the walls."

"What?" Cade looked at his aunt. What issue?

"The rose room will make her skin look rosy. How will we tell if the fever's gone?"

"If she were staying, we could use a thermometer," he said, standing. "But the issue won't arise because she's not staying."

"Cade, you can't send an ill woman out into a storm like this. I won't hear of it."

"Aunt Amelia, she's a total stranger. I know nothing about her. She came here from Florida. I'm sure she can make it as far as town, where she can get a motel room."

"I'll be on my way. I'm sorry for the problem I caused."

Jordan tried to stand, her knees feeling like soggy spaghetti noodles. She fell back to the sofa with a soft plop.

"See?" Amelia said triumphantly. "She can't possibly travel. If you don't wish to put her up, I will. It'd be crowded in the cottage, of course, but I won't shirk my duty to the less fortunate by sending a sick person out on a day like this!"

Cade suppressed the urge to roll his eyes at the familiar dramatic flare his aunt was famous for. He nodded once. He'd speak to Rosita for calling his aunt. If she hadn't arrived, he could have sent the stranger and her child on her way with no compunction.

Now he'd be stuck with her for at least a day. Hopefully, by tomorrow she'd be better and could head back to Florida.

"Then I'll leave her in you capable hands, Aunt Amelia."

"I'll take care of everything, Cade. You go on back to work. Ask Rosita to help me, will you?"

"She's busy right now with the little boy."

Amelia's eyes grew wide as saucers.

"Little boy? Why didn't you say so? Oh, it's been too long since this house has heard the ring of childish laughter. Where is he?"

"In the kitchen."

Yes, it had been too long since he'd heard childish laughter. It'd forever be too long.

She almost ran from the room in her quest to see the child.

Cade sighed and looked at the woman now sitting on the sofa, holding a hand against her chest, rubbing absently. The coughing had stopped. The bright spots of color in her cheeks attested to the fever.

She watched him with a wary expression. Except for the two spots of red staining each cheek with brilliant color, she was pale and wan.

"I'll leave in a few minutes. I can't stay here," she said.

"Amelia may invite whomever she wishes to stay. I can show you a bedroom large enough for you and your son. Or I can fix him up in another room, so he doesn't get whatever you have."

"If he were going to get it, four days in a car together would have exposed him," she said.

"It took you four days to get here from South Beach?"

She nodded. "We had car trouble."

Jordan watched him carefully, studying his features. He looked nothing like the college guy she'd fallen for. He was the wrong age, the wrong size, the wrong coloring and definitely not the man she'd want to tangle with.

"You've come a long way because of a newspaper article."

He waited for something more. The suggestion of help

she needed, maybe money for the return journey? Was she hoping for the sympathy play? Donations of that magnitude reported in the paper had already resulted in dozens of requests from other organizations.

Penny was fielding them all, but Jordan Carhart was the first individual to respond in person—that he knew of. Of course, Penny screened those as well.

"I thought it was fate. That I found Cade Cullen Everett just when I most needed him. He said he was from Texas. His family had a ranch. He told me stories about the place, but maybe it was all made up."

"When was this?"

"Five years ago. At spring break in South Beach."

"Wild spring break, fun parties and no responsibilities. You met him there?"

Jordan stiffened at the derision of his tone. What happened in her past was none of his business. She didn't need a stranger telling her how foolish she'd been.

Jordan rubbed her forehead again, her eyes closing. She wished she could find a bed and sleep for twelve hours.

"Life goes on. I'll get out of your way, Mr. Everett. Sorry to have bothered you."

"Stay the night, as Aunt Amelia suggested. The storm isn't easing and it'll be treacherous driving in it. If you aren't familiar with our roads, navigating them in a storm is to be avoided at all costs. Besides, the Circle E is known for its hospitality."

At least it had been when Marissa had been its mistress. She loved having friends over, entertaining, cooking for a crowd, and showing off the ranch.

No one had stayed the night since she'd been gone. Rosita would have to make the beds, air out the rooms as best she could with this storm.

He looked out the window. The wind had the trees bent under its force, while the rain was coming down in sheets. The last thing he wanted was some stranger and her appealing little boy in his house overnight. But his aunt was right. He wouldn't send anyone out in this—especially a sick woman and a child.

"Have you ever heard of another Everett family in Texas who has a ranch?" Jordan asked hopefully.

"As far as I know, there are no other Everett families who own ranches in Texas. I've been a member of the Cattleman's Association for years. I'm sure I'd have heard if there were others."

"He was blond, with bright blue eyes. Caleb got his eyes," she murmured. "Maybe the whole thing was a lie. For all I know, he's a druggist in New Jersey."

Slowly, she toppled over to her side.

"Though he did have a Texas drawl," she murmured as she succumbed to sleep.

"Well, blast it," Cade said softly as he watched her fall asleep.

Once Rosita had the room ready, Cade would rouse his uninvited guest, or carry her, let her sleep the night. If she wasn't better by morning, he'd call Paul again and have his friend come out.

But what in the meantime was he going to do with the boy?

He'd buried his wife and daughter. He'd never planned to be around children again. And he'd avoided family gatherings and made it clear to his sister and cousins he wasn't in the mood for company.

Amelia wanted them to stay. Let her entertain the child. She'd have her work cut out trying to amuse a young boy. But she was on her own. He would not become involved.

Maybe Jack Murray's wife could take charge of Caleb, if he proved too much for Amelia. The foreman's wife had raised three boys of her own, all out working on their own, now. She'd know what to do with one little boy.

And she'd relish the opportunity, while to him it'd cause only anguish.

He turned and strode from the room, angry at fate for interrupting his routine. He didn't need Penny going off. Didn't need Jordan Carhart or her cute little boy invading his life. And he sure didn't need to know someone had been impersonating him five years ago!

Chapter Two

J ordan awoke slowly and stretched beneath the covers. For the first time in ages, her headache was finally gone. She opened her eyes slowly, then sat up. A strange bed in a strange room. Where was she? This wasn't her bedroom, nor one of the anonymous motel rooms they'd stayed in on their way to Texas.

The sun shone from a clear sky. Through the tall windows dressed in crisp white Priscilla curtains, she could see the rolling Texas hills dotted with cattle.

Memory returned. She was at the Circle E Ranch. Vaguely she remembered talking with Cade Cullen Everett—only not her Cade Cullen Everett, some man they called Cade who looked nothing like the carefree college student whom she'd once loved.

She remembered Amelia and Caleb talking about horses and a stranger taking her temperature. Hadn't there also been an injection? It was all blurred. Had it been a dream?

Gingerly, she pushed back the light covers and rose, grabbing the headboard. She felt shaky. How sick was she? Her chest no longer hurt, her cough seemed gone.

The door opened and Rosita peeked in.

"Ah, you are awake. And getting up? That's good. I will tell Señorita Amelia and then bring breakfast."

Before Jordan could respond, she'd shut the door.

Jordan sat on the edge of the bed and looked around. Where was Caleb? How long had they been here? She seemed to remember various people popping in and out, but was that real or some dream? She saw her suitcase on a stand near the door. Rising again, she crossed over and found a clean set of clothes. Spying the en suite bathroom, she headed for it to shower and dress. She couldn't believe she'd stayed in a stranger's home.

Taking a deep breath, she felt relief. Her chest no longer hurt. Thank goodness for that. She'd dress, find Caleb, and be on their way. The trip had been for nothing. She still hadn't found the man she was searching for. The disappointment threatened to overwhelm her. Not only wouldn't they get the funds needed for the operation, she'd used several hundred dollars from the operation savings for this futile trip.

By the time she finished dressing, Jordan wanted to crawl back into bed and sleep another twenty-four hours. But Rosita had set up a lovely breakfast at the small round table by the tall windows. A light omelet was centered on the plate, fresh fruit beside it. A tall glass of orange juice and a cup of fragrant coffee completed the meal. She didn't know where to begin.

Where was Caleb? She sipped the orange juice and wondered if she should take the time to eat before seeking her son. She'd relinquished his care to Rosita yesterday, certainly a few more minutes might not hurt. And she was famished.

She ate slowly, savoring each delicious bite. A delightful

omelet, she thought, enjoying the blend of unknown spices and peppers. She'd ask for the recipe before she left.

They needed to get moving. Her week's vacation would be over before they returned home at the rate they were going. Though she hoped to make better time returning. Fingers crossed the car didn't break down again.

She could ill afford to keep it repaired. Every dollar she spent on the trip meant that much taken from their operation account. She was farther behind than when they'd started. She'd been so sure she'd find Caleb's father. Now what was she going to do?

A soft knock on the door presaged Amelia's arrival. Today she wore a soft rose dress, lace at the neck and on the cuffs of the sheer, long sleeves. Ballet slippers completed the ensemble, and she seemed to float along as she crossed the room to the table.

"Oh, you are awake at last. I'm so glad. How are you feeling? We've been so worried about you. But Paul said you'd be fine, just needed lots of rest and nourishment. And he gave you a shot since you couldn't take a pill with all your coughing. But the broth Rosita kept fixing didn't seem like enough food and you wouldn't ever drink it all. I think a nice poached egg would have been divine, but Cade said the broth would have to do."

Amelia took the chair opposite and beamed at Jordan.

"And Caleb is such a treasure. He brings so much delight. It's been too long since this house had a child in it. Of course, we all miss Vicki dreadfully, but she's been gone two years. And I think a big house deserves lots of children running through it, don't you? We had seven in our family. Mama said that was six too many sometimes, but she loved us all dearly. And we all loved her and Papa dearly. My younger sister married Bradley Everett. They're Cade's parents. The ranch belongs to Bradley, of course, though Cade runs it now that his parents are traveling. It's been in their family for generations. I have a small cottage in the back. Isn't Rosita's omelet delicious? I do like a spicy omelet. But of course, I cook for myself most of the time, only coming over to join Cade when he's here. Or when he travels if Rosita has made something special for dinner."

Jordan tried to follow the conversation, feeling her head spin at the rapid pace of Amelia's change of topics. When the woman took a breath, Jordan interrupted.

"Where's Caleb?"

"He's out with the horses. The child is crazy for them. If he were staying, I'd bet he'd be riding before you knew it. Vicki rode when she was only three. Of course, Cade got her a safe pony. He gave it away after her death. But he would never take a chance with a child, so if you were to stay, I'm sure he'd get another quiet pony for Caleb. Not that he's had much to do with the child. He has closed his heart to most things, living for work alone. He's increased the family coffers substantially, so none of us are complaining, but it would be nice to see him settled again. And not so driven."

Jordan assumed the Vicki she spoke of was the daughter who had died. Hearing about her made her even more real. She couldn't even imagine the full anguish of losing a child. It had to be the greatest heartache there was.

"There," Amelia said, beaming as Jordan ate the last bite of omelet. "It was delicious, wasn't it? I'm so glad to see you eating at last."

Jordan looked at her. "At last?"

"Four days with nothing but broth makes a person very weak, don't you think?" Amelia tilted her head as she looked at Jordan.

"*Four days?* I've been here four days?"

Jordan was horrified. She couldn't have imposed on total strangers for four whole days!

Cade couldn't believe one slightly snide comment would cause tears, histrionics and a slammed door. The temp had left in a flurry, leaving him alone in the front office, trying to make some sense of Penny's filing process. He pulled out another folder, glanced inside, and replaced it. Maybe he should pull in one man off the ranch. They at least wouldn't take offense at the slightest thing.

His secretary hadn't called to give him an estimated return date. He was growing impatient with the temps the sole agency in town was sending. Two in three days. Couldn't they find the right person—someone competent enough to do routine office tasks? Or if not that, at least someone who wouldn't take off at the first hint of complaint?

A small sound alerted him he was no longer alone. Cade glanced up and saw Caleb Carhart standing in the doorway.

"Kids aren't allowed in the office," Cade said.

He had a conference call in ten minutes and hoped he could find the Montgomery folder before then.

"The lady was saying bad words," Caleb said, walking in.

"I heard," Cade said.

Maybe he shouldn't have asked if she knew the alphabet in such a sarcastic manner. But blast it all, that folder was important and she hadn't been able to find it. Not that he was having much better luck.

Maybe his remark had been made in haste.

"Mommy never says bad words. She says we can be more creative and show we're smarter than people who copy other people to say bad words," he said solemnly.

Cade looked at Caleb. Hadn't he told the boy no kids allowed in the office?

"Is Mommy going to get better today?" Caleb asked, coming closer.

"I don't know. Probably."

Ah, the folder he'd wanted. Cade pulled it free and returned to his desk. He opened it, then looked at Caleb, who had moved to press against his side, peering in curiosity at the things on the wide surface of his desk.

"Look, kid, I have work to do. We have a policy against children being in the office."

"Mr. Murray said since my mommy is sick, I have to ask you if I can ride. I really want to be a cowboy. Can I ride one of your horses?"

Cade shook his head. "No."

Caleb didn't pester him like Vicki would have at the refusal. He merely hitched his shoulders a little and looked disappointed.

Cade studied him covertly. The kid was well behaved and not a pest. Jack said he ate up every word any of the cowboys said, and hung for hours on the corral fence talking to the horses and petting any that ambled his way.

Darn shame about his eyes. What was his mother going to do about that? It wasn't fair to the kid to have that kind of problem and not have the adults in his life take care of it.

Just then, Jordan Carhart rushed into the office.

"Mr. Everett, I didn't know I've been here this long," she said.

"Mommy!"

Caleb brightened instantly and ran to her.

The phone rang.

"Caleb."

She swung him up into her arms, hugging him close.

"Are you all better?" he asked.

"Everett," Cade said into the phone, watching Jordan and her son. The images blurred and he saw Marissa swing up their daughter. She'd adored Vicki. He'd loved them both so much. Missed them every day.

He turned away, forcing his gaze to move to the folder, ignoring the scene unfolding near the office door. He had work to do and the sooner he became involved, the sooner the piercing pain would fade.

"Cade says I can't ride. Can you get me a horse?" Caleb asked his mother.

Conscious of her reluctant host on the phone, she stepped into the outer office.

"Shh, he's busy. No, we can't get a horse. We need to get back home. Joe's going to be mad as it is. I'm already late returning to work and haven't even let him know we're still in Texas."

"I like it here."

"Home is best," Jordan said, relishing the feel of her little boy.

He struggled to get down. She never got to hold him as long as she wanted anymore. He was growing up too fast.

Glancing around, Jordan was amazed at the high-tech feel to the office. Amelia's rambles had included information about Cade, and every other person in a twenty-five-mile radius, she suspected.

But it was the newly gained knowledge that Cade ran the family holdings that had fascinated her. She'd thought he was a rancher, and while Amelia assured her he lived for part of the year on the ranch, he also had penthouse apartments in Los Angeles, New York and Dallas. According to Amelia, it was nothing unusual for Cade and his personal assistant to take off on short notice for one or the other city when business demanded.

"Want to come see the horses, Mommy?" Caleb asked, struggling to be let down.

She put him on his feet and brushed his cheek. Leaning against the desk, she shook her head.

"Not just yet. I want to talk to Mr. Everett."

She glanced through the opened door and wondered how long he'd be on the phone. She felt embarrassed to have stayed so long in his house. While she still felt a little shaky, she knew she'd infringed on his hospitality long enough. After thanking him, she'd pack Caleb's things and head back for Florida. Her suitcase was all ready to go.

"Can I go see the horses?" Caleb asked. "Mr. Murray said it's okay as long as I stay out of the corral. I just climb up the fence. I never go inside the corral."

"Is that what you've been doing while I was sick?" Jordan asked, brushing back his hair.

How could she have been unaware of the passage of four days?

He nodded, his eyes shining.

"Okay, then, if it's all right with those in charge. But we aren't staying long. We have to get back home. As soon as I speak with Mr. Everett, we'll be on our way."

His face fell. "Do we have to? I love it here. They've got horses and cows and dogs and even a cat in the barn, but I can't pat her because she doesn't much cotton to people."

Jordan almost laughed at Caleb's phrasing. Who had he been talking to?

"Then run along and say your goodbyes."

Jordan watched Caleb scamper away. Hearing Cade's voice in the background, she suspected his call would last a few minutes. Tired, she moved to sit in the chair behind the desk. She still felt weak.

And mortified that she'd been four days imposing on these kind people. How could she have been so sick?

According to Amelia, the doctor had said it was borderline pneumonia. They must think her crazy to show up at their front door so ill. But she'd truly thought it was a cold.

She'd offer to reimburse Cade for their expenses. It'd take even more from the operation fund, but that couldn't be helped. She wouldn't be beholden to anyone. Her aunt Maggie had harped on that all the years Jordan lived with her.

Closing her eyes, she rested her head on the back of the

chair. As soon as she'd finished with Cade Everett, she'd find a motel in Tumbleweed and stay another day to rest up. By then, she'd be ready for the drive home.

She'd better call Joe and make sure he knew she hadn't disappeared off the face of the earth. And a quick call to her friend Julie, too. She'd be eager to know the outcome of the trip.

Thinking of all she had to do, Jordan slowly drifted off to sleep.

Cade hung up the phone, satisfied with the conversation. If Jim followed up as he'd promised, Cade wouldn't have to take a trip to LA anytime soon.

Tossing the folder to the corner of the desk, he reached for the phone to call the temp agency. Tumbleweed wasn't large enough to support more than one agency, and their selection of potential employees was slim. Too bad. They'd just have to find someone else. The two they'd sent hadn't worked out.

He heard a chair squeak. Curious, he rose and crossed to the outer office. Jordan Carhart was asleep in Penny's chair. She was listing slightly to the left, and if she continued her slow slide, she'd fall over.

He reached out and shook her shoulder lightly. When she opened her eyes and looked up at him in sleepy confusion, he felt an odd unfurling deep within.

She looked young, innocent, and unaware of where she was. Her hair was a soft cloud of gold around her face, soft and silky. Her eyes shimmered in silvery lights.

For a moment Cade yearned to touch that hair, to sift it

through his fingers and feel its silken weight, let it flow around his hand like gossamer. To stare into the silvery pools of her eyes and forget all of yesterday's heartaches.

He frowned and jerked his hand away. What was he thinking? She was a troublesome visitor, nothing more. And he wanted nothing to do with any woman. He'd loved his wife. Her death had devastated him. He refused to become involved again, even superficially. Death was too final, a parting too painful.

"I'm sorry," she said, standing abruptly. "I fell asleep again. You must think I'm crazy. Usually I have tons of energy."

"You've been very sick. Should you even be up today?" he asked, studying her closely.

"I'm fine. Actually, we'll be leaving soon. I wanted to thank you for all your help. I'm, um, I wanted to reimburse you for any—"

He shook his head and stepped away before her light fragrance muddled his brain.

"No need. I hope you have a pleasant journey home."

She smiled uncertainly.

"Thank you. If you ever hear of another Cade Cullen Everett, would you let me know? I'll leave my address and phone number."

He looked at her for a long moment. What were the chances of there really being another Cade Cullen Everett? Had she come to attempt a scam? If so, why hadn't she followed through? Nothing had been said, nothing even hinted.

If she was trying to run a con, she sure had a long way to go. Caleb had mentioned getting money for his eyes, but Jordan Carhart had never raised the subject.

Maybe she was just what she said she was, a young mother searching for her child's father.

"If I ever hear of another man with my name, I'll let you know."

Jordan held out her hand.

"Thank you again, Mr. Everett. I appreciate all your hospitality."

He shook her hand, surprised at the sensation he experienced when he touched her. Her hand was cool, firm in his. She didn't hold on, never tried to flirt, but the jolt of awareness was real.

"Tell me why you came here, Jordan Carhart," he said on a impulse. "Caleb said something about an operation for his eyes."

She nodded, raising her chin slightly.

"I know you've seen how they are crossed. The insurance I have doesn't cover the cost for the operation, so I have been saving almost since he was born to pay for it." She shrugged. "When I saw the article in the newspaper about your family donating money to the Last Wish Foundation, I thought I'd found Caleb's father. I thought—"

He waited a moment when she went silent.

"Thought you'd hit him up for it," he finished for her.

She flushed slightly.

Cade stared. He couldn't remember the last time he'd seen a woman blush. It didn't go with the image he'd formed, of a swinging single woman partying at the beach who had gotten caught with a baby.

"I'm only a couple of thousand short, I thought if he, you…I mean, I thought it was Caleb's father who donated so much. And if he had that much to donate, then he could surely spare two thousand dollars for his own son." She ended all in a rush. "Caleb's really a great little boy. And I hate for him to start school with the problem."

Cade rubbed the back of his neck. The few times he'd seen Caleb, the kid had been upbeat and enthusiastic. He'd worried about his mother, then scampered off and been captivated by the horses. Jack reported he was no trouble, and was, in fact, soaking up everything he learned.

Cade could understand Jordan's determination. If Vicki had needed anything, he would have moved heaven and earth to get it for her. He turned and went to the door, looking out over the spread.

He hadn't been able to do anything for his daughter. By the time he'd heard of the drunken driver crashing into his wife's car, both Marissa and Vicki had been dead for several hours.

But maybe he could help another child.

He turned and glanced around the room.

"Do you know anything about office work?" he asked.

Chapter Three

"Not much," Jordan said, surprised at the question. Waiting tables was nothing like working in an office.

"Can you type, answer the phones?" he persisted.

She thought about the hours she's spent on the Internet searching for Caleb's father while Caleb enjoyed storybook time in the library. About the endless letters she'd typed on the library computers and sent out—always searching.

"I can type, but not fast. And anyone can answer a phone."

"I need clerical help," he said. "Penny, my personal assistant, had to leave on a family emergency a few days ago. I've had two incompetent women in since then, and the office is in more chaos than if I had had no one."

"I have a job waiting for me in South Beach," Jordan said.

"I'll make you a deal. I'll make up the difference for Caleb's surgery and he can have the operation in Dallas. In exchange, you work for me until Penny returns."

That would solve the problem of a temp leaving in a huff.

Jordan stared at the man. He would pay for the surgery for a total stranger? What was the catch?

"How long is Penny going to be gone?"

"I do not know, a couple of weeks, a couple of months. She's supposed to let me know when she has a better handle on things at her end. Do we have a deal?"

Jordan bit her lip, hope flooding. Did he mean it? He'd pay the balance for Caleb's surgery if she worked in his office until Penny returned? Could she get Joe to hold her job until she got back to Florida?

Did she even care about that job if she got Caleb's surgery taken care of? Good waitresses weren't as plentiful as people thought. She'd be able to get another job if Joe wouldn't take her back.

The thought of having Caleb's eyes fixed before he started school made her almost giddy.

"Just office work?" she clarified. He wasn't expecting anything else, was he? Not that she was some femme fatale, but his offer seemed too generous for mere clerical work—especially for someone who had no office experience.

His PA could return before the surgery was even scheduled. Then what?

"I have a housekeeper. I don't need another one. And Amelia doubles as hostess when I have a need for one for business events. I only need help with office work," Cade replied.

"I won't be fast or as efficient as a trained office worker," she warned.

Was she an idiot? She should snap up his offer in a heartbeat.

The offer seemed too good to be true. There had to be a hidden string attached somewhere. But Jordan didn't care. The fact Caleb would have his operation was all that mattered to her.

"I have several thousand dollars saved up. I'll have my bank transfer it out here," she said. "I don't need the entire operation paid for, just the difference from what I have saved."

"I said I'd take care of the bill. You keep your money," Cade said. "We can settle all that after the operation. Are you up to starting now?"

"I can't believe you'd offer to do this for me. For Caleb."

Cade narrowed his gaze as he looked at her.

After a long moment, he said, "I'm doing it for Vicki."

The phone rang.

Jordan looked at it, then at him.

"I start now?"

He hesitated, studying her pale features.

"Work until lunch, then rest up this afternoon. Time enough tomorrow to put in a full day." He nodded toward the phone, "Answer it—Everett Enterprises."

She picked up the phone, her voice rich and firm as she identified the business. She had seen enough television to know how topnotch professionals acted. Too bad her faded jeans and loose top weren't sophisticated apparel. That definitely ruined any competent image she could hope to give.

She covered the receiver.

"A Mr. Baker from a bank."

"I'll take it in my office."

Jordan held the receiver to her ear until she heard Cade pick up, then hung up her phone. The vast array of buttons and numbers on the console phone had her confused.

Of course, a business office would have several phone lines. Was there an instruction booklet somewhere to give her a clue on how to use the thing?

She sat back down, feeling breathless and excited. Cade Everett was going to see to Caleb's operation. Her son's eyes would be completely normal within weeks.

It felt as if an enormous weight lifted from her shoulders at the generosity of one man.

But why was he doing this? Surely he could hire help with no trouble. Why pay what would be the equivalent of an exorbitant fee for the length of time she'd be working?

And where was she going to live in the meantime? Who'd take care of Caleb while she worked? He couldn't run wild around the ranch.

She had to call Joe. She needed to call Julie, her best friend, to tell her where she was, all that had happened. Maybe listen to a word of warning.

Jordan knew Vicki had been Cade's daughter. Amelia had regaled her with enough stories about the little girl that Jordan felt she'd known her.

Suddenly she frowned. She'd have to do the best job she could. She hoped his helping Caleb would ease some of the pain from his daughter's loss.

Since Cade seemed to spend most of his time on the phone that morning, Jordan had gone through every drawer and file in Penny's desk by lunchtime, halfway feeling as if she were trespassing.

But Jordan wanted to do the best she could, so tried to

learn as much as she could about how the office operated. Even so, she'd never be able to repay Cade Everett for the gift he was giving.

She scrolled through a list of names and numbers she found on the computer, wishing Penny had provided background on each person. Especially the notations that had only first names, like Hank or Sara.

Jordan had excellent recall. She often took the orders from a large group without aid of a notepad. If Cade asked her to call someone, she knew she'd remember if their name had been on the list.

She scrolled through some other files on the computer, getting a feel for how he liked his letters, the kinds of correspondence he had his PA handle.

She didn't find a booklet to show her how to use the phone. Trial and error would have to suffice, she thought fatalistically when she disconnected a caller.

If Cade Everett wanted her to know how to run the phone, he'd have to show her or let her learn as she went.

A separate phone, a single line, rang. Jordan lifted it.

"Everett Enterprises," she said brightly.

"Hi, Mommy. Rosita said I could call you to see if you're coming to lunch. She made tacos and salad and other stuff."

Jordan glanced at the clock. It was almost one.

"Yes, I could go for some lunch. I'll be right there."

The morning hours had flown by.

Cade was on the phone—again. It hadn't stopped ringing since that first call. She'd found the message pads and carefully wrote the names and numbers. Getting jumbled up on two messages, she figured he'd know what the call was about.

Did she just leave for lunch? Should she let him know she was leaving?

She went to the door to his office, the stack of phone messages in hand. He looked up and covered the receiver with his hand.

"Do you need something?" he asked.

"Caleb called and said Rosita had prepared lunch."

"Bring me back a plate."

With that, he resumed his phone conversation.

She placed the stack of notes on his desk and took off.

Jordan savored the warm sunshine as she crossed from the office to the main house. The sky was cloudless. The scent of dried grass and a hint of cattle and horses filled the air. What a difference from the downpour when they arrived.

She could hardly believe all that had transpired since that afternoon. First, Cade had not been the man she was looking for. Then she'd fainted away like some Victorian wimp, which made her feel totally a flake.

Being sick was not deliberate, but she still couldn't believe the hospitality of the Everetts to put her up for four days. And instead of demanding compensation, Cade was going to pay for Caleb's surgery. It all seemed like a dream. Would she awaken soon and find she was late for work at Joe's Fish Tacos?

However, walking up the steps into the house, Jordan felt exhausted. Not that she'd admit that to anyone. She didn't want Cade to think she wasn't up to the job and withdraw his offer. She hoped the midday meal would perk her up—maybe even enough to finish the day in the office.

Or it might be better to take Cade up on his offer to take the afternoon off. She had to make plans for their stay in Texas. Hopefully Amelia would suggest a reasonably priced apartment complex. If she didn't return to work today, she could drive into Tumbleweed and find accommodation.

And a day care center for Caleb.

There were tons of things to do, but none of them seemed insurmountable. After all, her darling little boy would soon have his eyes fixed.

Amelia and Caleb were already seated at the large dining room table when Jordan joined them.

"Cade not coming?" Amelia asked, peering behind Jordan.

"He's on the phone, asked if I'd bring a plate. Should I take it first?"

"No, dear. Sit down and eat. You look pale. Maybe you should take a long nap this afternoon. You just got up this morning for the first time in four days. My mother always said a woman needed to look after herself because the menfolks surely wouldn't."

"Tacos, Mommy," Caleb said, holding up a crisp corn tortilla filled with meat, lettuce and cheese.

"It looks delicious, sweetie."

Jordan sat where Amelia indicated and soon had her own plate filled with a delicious taco salad. Rosita had made the traditional tacos for Caleb. Jordan was surprised and touched at the extra effort the housekeeper had gone to for her son.

"Come with me to see the horses after lunch," Caleb said.

"Your mother needs to rest," Amelia said emphatically.

"Oh, I can't. Cade hired me to work in the office until his PA gets back. I don't have time for a nap. There's so much to do."

"Nonsense. You're exhausted, I can tell. A quick nap is important. I'll tell the man myself."

Visions of being fired before the day ended flashed through Jordan's mind.

"I'm fine. Lunch will give me plenty of energy. And I'm grateful for the job. I don't want to jeopardize it."

"Aunt Amelia said she'd go with me to the horses, can't you, too?" Caleb said.

"Caleb. She's not your aunt."

"I asked the child to call me aunt. It's little enough. I so love children. I loved being around while Cade and his sister and cousins were little. Vicki was such a darling precious child."

"It must be so hard to lose a child," Jordan murmured.

"It is, even one not my own. She's been dead these two years now. Their car was broadsided by a drunken driver when she was eight. She and Marissa never had a chance, the police said."

Amelia shook her head in sorrow.

"I truly didn't think Cade would survive. When he heard, he went crazy. Then he just closed himself off from everything."

Jordan's gaze moved to Caleb, her own precious child. What would she do if something happened to him? How would she survive?

If closing himself off worked for Cade, more power to him. She thought she'd probably die herself from a broken heart.

"Vicki was almost as horse crazy as Caleb. She loved to ride. She had the sweetest pony. A lot of ponies aren't sweet, don't you know? But this one was. And she followed her dad around whenever he was home. Marissa could only have the one child and they both doted on her."

"Cade offered to pay the balance for Caleb's operation," Jordan said, "saying it was for Vicki."

Amelia looked surprised.

"Did he? How unexpected." She reached for more iced tea. "He always had a soft spot for kids. But since Vicki died, he's made it clear he doesn't want his niece or nephew visiting for long, or any of his cousins' children. I think their presence reminds him too strongly of Vicki's death."

Amelia regaled them with funny stories of the younger generation and the antics they got into on the ranch. It helped lighten the mood.

"I'll need to find a place to stay. Maybe you can give me some suggestions of where to look in Tumbleweed," Jordan said a little later when they were almost finished lunch.

"I wouldn't hear of it. You and Caleb need to stay right here. I can watch him myself while you work. And Rosita loves children. She has seven herself and four grandchildren already. Besides, staying here will save time driving back and forth. If Caleb's having an operation, he'll need care while he recovers, so where better than right here?"

Amelia beamed at Jordan, then winked at Caleb.

Her rose-colored dress was the perfect foil for her snowy white hair and pink cheeks. Jordan could feel the honesty in the woman's tone and actions. Amelia genuinely liked people and sincerely wanted to help.

Jordan had the feeling Amelia would have done well as a hostess for some rich ranch owner in the earlier days. She loved flowery, feminine clothes, had a graciousness about her that was endearing. And she loved children. What better person to watch her son when Jordan could not?

Except Jordan couldn't let her.

What would Cade say when he heard of his aunt's invitation? The job hadn't come with an offer of room and board.

Jordan needed to be independent. And she couldn't infringe any longer on these people's generous hospitality.

She finished lunch quickly, promising to go see the horses with Caleb once she had a chance. Taking a covered plate from Rosita, she hurried back to the office. Lunch had given her renewed energy. She still felt tired, but not too tired to slack off.

Cade stood by the printer when she entered, watching as page after page rolled out.

Jordan studied him for a moment before he realized she'd returned. She attributed the lines around his mouth to sadness. Was the solemn way he viewed life as a direct result of the blows life had dealt?

How sad he pushed other family members away. They might help him remember the good times and get past the immediate pain of loss.

Amelia said it had been two years—not that there was a time limit on grieving. But he needed to move on and find happiness where he could.

Jordan knew this from the death of her own parents, and more recently, Aunt Maggie. She had only Caleb. She'd have welcomed family rallying around when her elderly aunt died.

Cade looked up and caught her gaze, then saw the plate. "Thanks. I'm hungry."

"Rosita piled it high, saying you needed to eat it all."

"If I ate all Rosita gave me, I'd need to bunk in the barn. None of the beds in the house would hold me."

Jordan grinned. Maybe he wasn't such a somber man after all.

"I can watch the papers for you if you want to eat. Will the machine jam?"

"No, I'm just waiting for the full report so I can read it."

"Go eat, I'll bring it in when it's all here," she said, holding out the plate.

Cade took it and went into his office. He was hungry enough to eat everything Rosita had sent. As he ate, he looked into the outer office. By angling his chair just so, he could see Jordan standing by the printer. She was faithfully watching each sheet as it came out, taking it and stacking it with the rest. Her jeans were loose on her. Had she lost weight because of being ill, or was she naturally thin?

A few weeks of Rosita's food and she'd plump up a bit.

He looked away. He didn't care if she did or didn't fill out. She was merely a stranger who was going to help him out until Penny came back. A stranger with silky blond hair and sparkling silvery eyes. Her skin was flawless, and surprisingly pale for someone who lived in a beach town in Florida. Or was it because of her recent illness?

He took another bite of the spicy taco salad and tried to banish his thoughts. He didn't care what she did or didn't do in Florida. As long as she didn't fly out of here in a huff like the last two temps, he'd be satisfied.

She brought in the printed pages, placing the stack near the plate on the desk.

He nodded, but she didn't leave. When he looked at her, she appeared nervous.

"Something wrong?" he asked.

"I don't think so."

She cleared her throat, glanced down at the report, then met his eyes.

"Your aunt invited us to stay here while I'm working for you. I asked her to recommend a place in town where we could live but she insisted we plan to remain here. I'm sure room and board aren't in the deal, so maybe you could recommend a place for us to look at in Tumbleweed. I could try to get something lined up this afternoon."

He'd never thought about housing. Of course, she had no place to stay in Texas. She was from Florida.

If she had to get a place in town, it'd have to be furnished, inexpensive and without a lease. Nothing like that came to mind.

There was the added worry about who would watch her son—especially after the surgery, when Cade was sure he'd have to be kept quiet for a while. Jordan Carhart knew no one in town. How would she keep her mind on business when a stranger was watching her convalescing child?

Amelia and Rosita would spoil the child in their delight to watch him.

"Staying here makes the most sense," he said. "If you don't like the lilac room, ask Rosita to give you another."

She looked at him as if he'd lost his mind.

"I can't stay here."

He leaned back in his chair.

"Why not?"

"You're already doing so much. I can't take room and board as well."

She certainly wasn't running some scam. He'd been around his fair share of proud, determined women. Marissa had been very independent. Now this. Try to do a good deed and have to argue about it.

Do a good deed? Where had that come from?

He was merely helping a child who needed it. It was easy to throw money at a problem. And he had it to spare. Not that it meant a thing. All the money in the world wouldn't have saved Vicki or Marissa.

Thinking about them usually brought their images to mind. But now he only saw Jordan.

"I have to read this report and draft a response. We'll need to get it emailed back today. Look for the Milford file. The temp couldn't find it or any of the others I asked for. How hard can it be?"

Jordan looked as if she wanted to argue the point of staying, but he had ended the discussion. She was smart enough to pick up on that.

Cade relaxed slightly when she went to the file cabinets in her office and opened drawer after drawer. He could hear them slam shut. So the lady had a temper. She looked so sweet and young and feminine he hadn't expected that. She'd learned to control that temper somewhere. He hadn't picked up a clue until she slammed the drawers. What would it be like to let loose? Did that passionate feeling spill over into other areas? Like when she was involved with a man?

Chapter Four

B y dinnertime, Jordan's spirits were high. She'd worked a couple of hours in the office after lunch, arranged to visit the doctor with Caleb the next afternoon and taken a nap at Amelia's insistence.

She was feeling resigned to staying at the Everett Ranch until Cade's PA returned and falling in with Amelia's desires to watch Caleb. She had mixed emotions—not wanting to be beholden to strangers, and yet incredibly grateful for the chance to have Caleb's eyes operated on sooner than she'd thought possible.

She wished she'd brought more than just a couple of changes of shorts and slacks, but hadn't expected to spend any more time with Caleb's father than it took to have him meet Caleb and agree to help with the operation.

Amelia always wore flowery dresses, which were a bit excessive, Jordan thought privately, but at least she dressed up for dinner. Jordan had to wear her same old slacks and shirt.

Still, Jordan's clothes were freshly laundered, thanks to Rosita. And Caleb was clean from a bath and a change of clothes.

When they entered the dining room, Amelia had already

taken her seat at the foot of the table.

"There you two are. Do sit. I thought one on either side, to balance the table. Cade will be here soon. We'll begin once he arrives. I hope you have an appetite tonight. Rosita has been cooking all afternoon. Did you sleep well, dear?" she asked Jordan.

"The nap was lovely, thank you," Jordan responded, helping Caleb into the indicated chair, then going around the table to take her seat.

The dining room was more formal than they were used to. Jordan hoped Caleb's manners would hold up. Sometimes a four-year-old forgot.

Cade entered at that moment, hesitating in the doorway as he looked at the three people already there. For a second, Jordan thought he might turn and leave. Should she have eaten in the kitchen with Rosita?

He moved swiftly to the place at the table's head and sat, to her relief. She'd hate to cause dissension in his household.

"I didn't realize we'd all be eating together," he murmured with a look at his aunt.

"Now that Jordan's out of bed and feeling so much better, I knew you'd want us all to have our meals together. It's fine for Caleb to eat with Rosita from time to time, but there's no need now that his mother's no longer sick. He needs to eat with family. I think Jordan looks much better, don't you? She was so pale the afternoon they arrived," Amelia said gaily.

She was obviously pleased at the dinner arrangement.

Jordan felt warmth steal into her cheeks as Amelia continued. She darted a glance at Cade to find his dark eyes studying her gravely as his aunt talked about Jordan's recovery. Her heart beat rapidly, and she wondered if she'd made a mistake accepting this man's hospitality. She couldn't deny the spark of attraction she felt anytime she was in proximity to him. Not that she'd let that influence her behavior. She wasn't looking for any kind of relationship. Been there, done that. Now she had Caleb to think about as well.

Rosita entered, carrying bowls of vegetables and potatoes. Placing them in the center of the table, she returned in moments with a huge platter of fried chicken and a basket of fluffy biscuits.

Jordan remained feeling awkward after Cade's comment. She hoped they could eat quickly and leave him in peace.

He ate without comment, as if as eager to get finished and away from the table as she was. Tomorrow she'd suggest she and Caleb eat in with Rosita.

Amelia seemed to find nothing amiss with dinner and smiled at Caleb as he worked his way through the dinner.

"Tell us what you did today, Caleb," Amelia said. "I know we went to see the horses, but what else did you do?"

"Mr. Murray said I could watch the cat in the barn and he let me pat the dogs, but I can't play with them because they're working dogs and he doesn't want them spoiled," Caleb said solemnly.

"Oh pooh, those dogs know their jobs. A bit of fun with a little boy won't spoil them, will it Cade?" Amelia said.

He glanced at her. "Jack handles that Amelia."

"But you could tell him to let Caleb play with the dogs when they aren't working. Vicki did. A little boy needs to have a dog."

The tension at the table rose dramatically. Jordan held her

breath at the change, looking at Amelia in dismay. From the little she'd learned from the woman that morning, Cade had taken his daughter's death hard and didn't speak of her.

It almost seemed as if Amelia was pushing Jordan and Caleb at Cade—to replace his lost family. Jordan hoped she was misreading the situation. Nothing could be farther from her own reason for being here.

If Amelia became too pushy, she and Caleb would have to leave.

Cade pushed back his chair and rose.

"If you will excuse me." In two seconds, he had left the room.

"Oh dear, I shouldn't have said that. Cade's still so touchy about Marissa and Vicki. But I wanted Caleb to have the fun of playing with the dogs while he's here. Sophie is the dog Vicki used to play with. I think they have a couple of new ones that she never saw. But it doesn't matter. The dogs wouldn't hurt the boy and he couldn't possibly untrain them." Amelia shook her head, staring after her nephew. "He acts as if Vicki and Marissa never existed. I miss them, too. We all do. But I remember the good times, and wish I had someone to share them with," she said sadly.

Jordan knew staying would be impossible with the situation the way it was. Kind as Amelia had been, she couldn't remain. She'd have to find accommodation on her own, preferably before Cade asked her to leave. She only hoped that he'd let her keep the job. She couldn't bear it if he snatched that away just when she thought he could help Caleb.

Once they had finished dinner, Jordan took Caleb to his bedroom.

"In the morning, we're going to look for a nice apartment

in Tumbleweed," she said, sinking on the edge of his bed. He'd been given the rose room. She looked around, admiring the decorations, knowing a small boy would be happier with fewer things to knock against or stay away from.

"Can we get a dog?" he asked, leaning against her leg.

Jordan brushed back his light brown hair and shook her head regretfully.

"No, we won't be here that long. When we go back home, I'll see if the apartment manager will let us get a dog. How's that?"

"And a horse?"

Jordan laughed and hugged her son.

"Not a horse. Goodness, it'll be crowded in our apartment with a dog. Where would we put a horse?"

Caleb laughed at her nonsense and offered several suggestions, each more outlandish than the other. Soon they were laughing together, as they often did. Love surrounded them.

Jordan savored the happy moment. She loved her son so much. How much of his life his father was missing. She wished she had found the man after searching for so long.

When she put him to bed sometime later, she kissed him and tucked him in.

"Sleep well, sweetie," she murmured, imagining how Cade must feel having lost his little girl.

For a moment, Jordan wanted to snatch Caleb up and hold him tightly away from harm for the rest of their lives. The worst nightmare—losing a child. How did Cade stand it?

She went back downstairs. The house was quiet. Lights

were on in the living room and down the hall in the study. Jordan peered into both rooms. They were empty.

She turned to go back upstairs when something had her push open the front door and step out into the wide veranda.

Cade sat in one of the chairs on the right, his legs stretched out, hands tucked into the pockets of his pants. It was dark, only the light from the living room spilled out to provide illumination.

"Are you asleep?" she whispered.

If he was, she'd tiptoe away.

"No."

The short answer wasn't very conducive to conversation. But what she had to say couldn't be delayed.

She walked closer, leaning against a column, gazing over the dark landscape. The lights were on in the bunkhouse and the barn, otherwise the ranch was cocooned in the velvet night. Stars shone as pinpoints of lights in the vast expanse of the black sky.

"I apologize for the awkwardness at dinner," Jordan started.

She wanted him to know it hadn't been her idea, without feeling she was trying to accuse Amelia.

"Aunt Amelia may invite whomever she wishes to dinner," he commented.

"We're leaving in the morning."

"What are you talking about?" he asked, rising.

In two steps he stood beside her.

Jordan looked up. His face was planes and shadows, but she knew he was staring down at her. Her breath caught in her throat, but she held firm.

"I'll still work for you, if that's what you want. And I'll be so grateful for the operation. I'll pay you back every cent."

"Unnecessary."

"But we can't stay here. It isn't fair to you."

He was silent for a long moment.

"I can decide what is fair for me. Stay."

She shook her head.

"I can't. We can't. It's too awkward, too painful."

"How?"

"I can see it in your eyes. You don't want Caleb around, no children. Amelia said you disappear when your sister and her children come. You've asked your cousins not to come to visit. It's because of Vicki. I understand, truly I do, which is why we need to leave. That way you won't be constantly reminded, won't have a rambunctious four-year-old underfoot all the time."

He turned and glared off into the night. The silence stretched out. Jordan wished she could ease the man's anguish, but there was nothing. She was about to turn to reenter the house when he spoke, his voice low and pain fulled.

"She was eight. *Eight.* She should have had another eighty years."

Jordan swallowed, longing to reach out and offer sympathy, not knowing if he would accept it. Words were so inadequate at a time like this.

"It's so tragic," she murmured. "I'm sorry. I wish I could change things."

"A senseless waste of two good lives."

"I know."

Tentatively, she reached out to touch his arm. He turned, hesitated a moment. Even in the dim light, she could see the intensity of his gaze. He leaned closer and Jordan held her breath. Was he going to *kiss* her?

Her heart raced. For the first time in years, she longed for the touch of a man's mouth against hers. She had dated only casually since her Cade Cullen Everett had left her life. None of the men had interested her long enough for a second or third date.

But this attraction that flared had her wishing for things that couldn't be. She almost leaned forward, just a few scant inches, to meet him halfway. To offer her mouth to his, hoping he'd kiss her and find some solace in the contact.

Startled at the thought, Jordan did nothing for several minutes, conscious of the tension that rose until she could almost reach out and touch it.

Finally, he turned with an expletive and headed out to the barn. Slowly she drew in a breath, unaware she'd been holding hers until he left.

She watched as he strode across the dark grass, his back ramrod straight and taut. He'd wanted to kiss her. She was sure of it. And she'd wanted him to.

Hadn't she learned anything from Cade Cullen Everett of South Beach?

Shivering with the closeness of the contact, she turned and fled into the house, afraid of the sensations that filled her, of the yearning for that one man that filled her. She had no business thinking of anything between them except business—and then only to repay the magnificent gift he was giving her.

"Blame it on the night and the company and the memories," she tried to tell herself as she got ready for bed. "He's a man, you're a woman, it was proximity, or the romantic feel to the night. He wasn't going to kiss you personally, just any woman to forget the pain he lives with every day. Men don't feel the same emotional ties as women," she reminded herself.

When she slipped between the sheets of her bed, she tried to convince herself. But a part of her still craved a kiss from Cade Everett.

"No harm done," she said. No harm? Maybe not, but for a brief moment she'd felt she was in reach of paradise. It made her sad to know it meant nothing to Cade. And that it wouldn't happen again.

Cade heard the door shut from the corral. He leaned against the top rail and watched the horses resting for the night. The silence was deafening. What had he been thinking, trying to find relief from the constant ache of Marissa's passing, of Vicki's death, by kissing a stranger? He wasn't into such activities.

He hadn't been with a woman since Marissa. Had kissed no one since her death. He certainly had no business thinking of Jordan that way.

He rubbed his face with both hands and shook his head in disgust. If her reasons for leaving hadn't already been strong enough, he'd just made sure she had a few more. She was a guest on the property, deserving of his care and protection. Not have to worry she'd have to fight off his advances.

He slammed the heel of his hand against the post, startling the horses. He couldn't deny the feelings in his gut— the desire he had for closeness, for a woman's touch. But it also felt like a betrayal to Marissa. Blast it all, why had Jordan stumbled onto his ranch? And who had been impersonating him five years ago?

Getting no answers, he turned and headed for the office. He'd get some work done, try to forget the way his life was going by reviewing every bit of information he had on the Hollister situation. And just maybe tomorrow he'd head for Los Angeles and take care of things himself.

He certainly couldn't make a bigger mess of that situation than he had with Jordan Carhart and her son.

By the time dawn broke on the horizon, Cade had consumed three pots of coffee, found a glitch they'd overlooked on the Hollister deal, and was dog tired. He left a batch of papers for Jordan to scan and send.

Before showering for the day, he'd take a ride to clear his head. And decide just how much he was willing to unbend to keep his temporary assistant and her son on the ranch. Maybe it'd be best for them to find accommodations in town.

But he knew he couldn't have her that far away.

Saddling his favorite horse, Cade rode away from the main barn. As he passed the house, he glanced at the room Jordan slept in. For a moment, he could swear he could feel her slim body against his. Would she be soft and sweet, her womanly curves fitted against his own harder body? He spurred the horse, trying to quell the image that wouldn't go away.

When Jordan entered the kitchen sometime later, she was surprised to see Caleb already dressed and eating breakfast.

"I didn't hear you get up," she said, leaning over to give him a kiss on his cheek as he shoveled cereal into his mouth.

"Hi Mommy. I was hungry."

"I can prepare your breakfast, Miss Carhart," Rosita said, turning from the stove. "What would you like?"

"Could I just eat here? With Caleb?" Jordan asked.

She wasn't sure of the protocol, but breakfast would be very comfortable in the sun-filled room and she wanted to spend time with her son, rather than in isolation in the dining room.

"Certainly. What would you like this morning? I have eggs ready to go, sausages warming, biscuits, and grits."

"All the above," Jordan said, slipping into the seat next to Caleb.

She was starving—must be from not eating much over the last few days.

"Maybe you can help me, Rosita. I need to find an inexpensive place to stay in Tumbleweed while we're here. But I don't want a lease. We'll only be here long enough for Caleb to have his operation and until Penny returns."

Rosita frowned.

"I thought you were staying here in the house. Miss Amelia told me so yesterday."

"I think it best if we stay in town."

Rosita raised her eyebrow in question.

"It is not extra work for me," she said slowly. "This is a

big house. It's nice to have more rooms in use, more people to look after. Sometimes I have little to do."

Jordan looked at Caleb, then back at Rosita.

"I think it's not as nice for Cade. We're invading his privacy, forcing him into situations he'd rather avoid."

"Ah." The older woman nodded gravely. "Perhaps because of the child, but time moves on. Maybe you and the boy are what Señor Everett needs to help him move on, as well."

"He's already doing so much for us. I hate to make things awkward," Jordan said.

"I'll give you the address for my friend Samantha Billing. She works in the real estate office in town. If there are any short-term rentals, she'll know of them. But you must check with Señor Everett first."

"Thank you. I'm sure he'll have no problem with you giving me your friend's contact information."

Glad to have that settled, Jordan ate quickly, asking Caleb how he got himself dressed.

"Aunt Amelia said a big boy like me could probably do it all by myself, and I did when you were sick. Now I can do it every day," he said proudly.

So that was who took care of him while she'd been out of it. She'd wondered if it had been Amelia or Rosita. Both women seem happy to have Caleb around. She only hoped they were up to his endless energy.

Bracing herself when she entered the office a little later, Jordan was momentarily disappointed to find Cade hadn't arrived. Or had he? There was a pile of papers on her desk, with cryptic notes attached to two stacks, and a separate note for her. With her work outlined, she had plenty to do.

Jordan felt a warmth invade her heart when she saw the first item on the note to her was he would be back by the time she needed to leave for the doctor's appointment he'd arranged.

He hadn't forgotten, but she had. No looking for an apartment today.

It took more than ten minutes for her to figure out how to use the printer to scan the pages he had put out for her. Jordan kept trying different buttons and sequences until the paper she'd stacked in the bin began feeding through.

In the meantime, the phone rang several times. Buoyed up by her success yesterday, she soon felt confident in not disconnecting people, and in getting the messages down as clearly as she could.

Cade strode into the room as the last page of the second stack was feeding through the scanner. For a moment, Jordan felt a flare of panic. Should she say something about last night or ignore it? After all, nothing had really happened. It only felt like her life had been on the edge of a precipice and she wasn't sure if she had fallen or not.

"Good morning," he said.

"Good morning."

Her heart fluttered, and she knew color rose in her cheeks. She'd always hated how that happened. Would she never outgrow that childish reaction? He didn't seem to notice, however, striding quickly through the outer office into his own.

He left the door open, and Jordan watched him sit behind the desk. He and Penny probably set the office up so they could talk back and forth if needed.

The phone rang again, and she answered.

"It's for you, a Joel Brady," she called.

She turned back to the files he'd left on her desk. She'd put them away and see what else he wanted done. He'd mentioned yesterday he was sending dictation tapes into the office in Dallas for his secretary there to transcribe.

When the phone rang again, she picked it up, noticing Cade was still on the first call.

"This is Harry in LA. Tell Cade I've heard of being cryptic before, but to send an email with eleven pages of blank paper is over the top. What am I supposed to do with this?"

"Blank? But there was writing on every sheet," she said, looking at the stack in front of her. "Who is this?"

"Harry in Los Angeles. This isn't Penny, is it? Where's Penny?"

"She's away. I'm filling in."

And not doing a very good job, Jordan thought guiltily. She looked at the two stacks. One had only five sheets, so she knew instantly which stack she'd have to redo.

"I'm new at this. I thought I scanned each page and saved it to the drive. Each page went through the machine."

"Nothing came through. Did you have the pages backward in the feeder? Try flipping them over and send again."

"I'll resend right away."

"Fine. Have Cade call me when he's free."

Jordan quickly recopied the pages, saving to a new file on the computer. This she attached to the email to the LA employee.

She wanted to do a good job to justify Cade's helping her with the operation, but she felt foolish not being able to handle a simple thing like scanning a few pages. With such incompetence, would he reconsider her working for him?

She wrote up the message and added the pink note to the growing stack. How did he have time to talk to all these people every day and still get other work done?

She looked up from her work and studied the man. He seemed tired, though he was still immaculately turned out. He glanced up just then and caught her gaze, holding it for a full minute. Jordan's heart pounded. She felt a fluttery awareness rise just as it had last night.

It was after eleven when Jordan tidied her desk to prepare for leaving. Through Cade's Dallas office, an appointment had been made with the specialist at two o'clock in downtown Dallas. Jordan wanted plenty of time to locate the doctor's offices.

Cade hung up the phone and walked out to the outer office, checking his watch.

"We should leave soon. We can grab a bite of lunch on the way."

"What?"

Was she missing something? Where was Cade going?

"I'm driving you and Caleb into Dallas."

Jordan was confused.

"I can manage. You have work to do."

Besides, she almost added, you want nothing to do with my child, or any child, you've made that clear.

"I worked last night, caught up on everything important. The phone calls can wait. I'll drop you off, pick you up when you're ready to leave. Paul said the exam and tests would take about two hours. I'll stop by the Dallas office while you are at the doctor's."

"I don't know what to say. Thank you."

His driving would mean she didn't have to chance her old car, didn't have to figure out where to go in a strange city, didn't have to worry about parking.

It also meant she could devote her attention to Caleb if he became nervous or upset. She was grateful to Cade for his offer.

Even more grateful when she was settled in the front seat of the luxury sedan he drove. Despite the humid heat, the temperature remained cool thanks to the environmental control. The tinted windows made it easier to watch the unfolding scenery as they sped quickly toward the city. The sun shone in a cloudless sky. It was such a difference from the rainy day she'd arrived. She took advantage to watch the landscape as it flew by.

Caleb had brought one of his books and was buckled into his car seat, happy to look at the pictures.

Jordan knew it'd take a while to reach Dallas. Was she supposed to keep quiet or make small talk? She fidgeted with her purse strap, uncertain how to behave. Normally, she was friendly and found it easy to talk with people, but Cade was different.

"How far from the doctor's office are your Dallas offices?" she finally asked, the silence too much to bear.

"Only a few blocks. I'll give you the office phone number. If you finish earlier than expected, call me. I can be there quickly."

"We could walk to the offices, give us a chance to see something of Dallas."

"No need. It's going to be hot, and your son would probably wilt in the heat."

"His name is Caleb," she said, wondering if she'd ever heard Cade call him by name.

"Caleb. He's five?"

"He'll be five his next birthday, but he's only four right now."

"Tall for his age."

"His father was tall."

Cade flicked her a quick glance.

"It must be tough, raising a child on your own."

"It has its rewards," she murmured.

It had it drawbacks as well, which is why she'd been trying to find Caleb's father since she'd first found out she was pregnant. All children should have both parents—even if they didn't live together. But she'd never found the man she'd searched for over the years.

"How old are you?"

"Twenty-three."

Cade looked startled. "That young?"

"How old did you think I was?"

"Older, though you don't look it. You were eighteen when

you got pregnant?"

"Seventeen, almost eighteen."

He uttered an expletive. "What was the guy thinking?"

She sighed.

"In retrospect, I suspect he wasn't thinking at all, just out to have fun. Spring break is wild in South Beach."

"How did you meet him?"

Jordan wondered why all the questions. Had the quietness of the drive bothered him as well? She doubted it—nothing seemed to bother Cade Everett.

"I was waiting tables for some extra money. I was a senior in high school and wanted a particular dress for the prom. I had to earn the money myself."

"Parents couldn't help? Or at least warn you about randy college guys?"

"My parents died when I was eight. I lived with my Aunt Maggie, who warned me, time and time again. But I thought I was in love. I'd never felt like that before. And he was very—attentive, I guess. It wasn't until he left I realized it had been only a fling on his part."

"After you knew you were pregnant?"

"I tried to find him. But never could."

"Until you saw the article."

"Yes, though I still haven't found my Cade Cullen Everett. You're nothing like him. Older for one thing."

And eons more mature. He had a presence that other men would envy. And probably had women yearning after him like love struck teenagers.

It was a good thing she was immune to his attraction. She

wouldn't be caught fantasizing a second time about romance and happily ever after. Reality was hard, and Jordan had learned that lesson well.

"Did you try private investigators?"

She laughed softly.

"I don't have that kind of money. I considered giving him up," she whispered, so her son wouldn't hear her. "But I just couldn't. Aunt Maggie wasn't keen on my keeping the baby, but she ended up being a terrific help. She loved him to bits."

"Past tense?"

"She died two years ago in a freak accident. A bus jumped the curb, slamming into several people waiting. She and another were killed, three more were badly injured. I miss her a lot."

What an understatement. Jordan had lost her mainstay when her aunt had died. But she had no choice but to move on. She had her son to care for.

"So it's just you and Caleb?"

Jordan nodded, pleased he'd said her son's name easily enough this time.

"So I know what it's like to lose someone you love," she added softly. "Life eventually moves on."

"Two someones it sounds like, your aunt, and Caleb's father."

"I guess," she said.

Cade flicked a glance her way. She was gazing out the window, apparently lost in thought. Thinking about Caleb's father? How could the man have disappeared without considering the consequences of his actions?

Did she still miss him with the intensity he missed Marissa?

Maybe he and Jordan had something in common. The other man wasn't in the picture, but he was. He frowned. Not that it meant anything. But he couldn't help feeling protective toward her.

She had come up against terrific odds, yet seemed content in her life, plunging ahead with the courage he admired. She hadn't asked for anything from anyone.

Yet she never gave up hope of finding Caleb's father. Was there anything he could do? Hire those private investigators she couldn't afford?

As the traffic grew heavier, Cade tried to ignore the spark of protectiveness that rose. He didn't owe Jordan or her son anything. The best thing would be to step back, distance himself from them and their situation before they grew to depend upon him. He knew that way lay danger.

He hadn't been able to keep his wife and child safe.

He could help a little, just enough to make things easier— not become involved.

When Cade dropped Jordan and Caleb off at the high-rise building which housed the doctor's office, he handed her his business card.

"Remember to call if you get out early. Otherwise, I'll be here at four."

"Thanks."

She gripped Caleb's hand and headed into the building without a backward glance. Cade ignored the urge to follow them, to be with her while she waited for the tests. He had work to do, and nothing to offer his uninvited guests.

At four exactly, Jordan and Caleb walked out onto the hot sidewalk. Her head was spinning.

"There's Cade." Caleb said excitedly, pointing to the car parked at the curb part way down the block.

"You should call him Mr. Everett," she admonished, following his finger and spotting the car.

She clasped his hand as they hurried toward it.

"Aunt Amelia calls him Cade. So do you, I've heard you."

"Unless he asks you to use his first name, it's more polite for a little boy to use a person's last name."

She opened the back door and fastened him in his car seat, then slid into her place in the front. She felt shaky and relished the comfort of the soft seats.

"How did it go?" Cade asked, not yet moving from their spot.

Dazed, Jordan looked at him.

"They can do the procedure on Friday and if it all goes well, he'll be able to go home on Monday. The bandages will remain for a couple of weeks, though, and he has to keep quiet. No running around."

She couldn't believe things were happening so swiftly. She knew it was because of Cade and his influence. Gratitude rose.

"Thank you. I never thought we'd have it done so soon."

"That's good, then," Cade said. Paul had come through. Cade had told him to pull any strings he could to expedite the procedure.

Jordan simply smiled as she nodded, tears filling her eyes.

"It's terrific. I can't thank you enough."

He frowned and started the car, pulling out into traffic before speaking again.

"No thanks needed. You're the first one who didn't dash out of the office the minute I complained about something, or yelled about a missing file. At least I have help until Penny returns."

Jordan nodded, blinking away the tears. To her, it was a wonderful gift. To Cade, it was merely an exchange for someone to help in his office at home.

But couldn't he have had one woman from the Dallas office drive out every day?

Chapter Five

Cade glanced again at the glow in Jordan's eyes and felt as if she'd touched him. For the first time in years, he forgot the past and remained in the present. Beginning to enjoy her wonder and delight, he frowned, not wanting to get caught up in that illusion of happiness. Life had a way of slapping one down just when things were looking up.

"I can't believe after all this time it's really going to happen," she said again. "He'll have to be calm and not do any leaning over for a month after the surgery. Which is going to be hard for a little boy. But then, everything should be healed and he'll be as normal as you or I."

"As every child should."

As Vicki had been, with her bright eyes and ready laughter. Vicki would have enjoyed showing her pony and the dogs to Caleb. She'd been such an outgoing child.

"I can't express how much I appreciate your paying for this. I'll pay you back, every cent."

"You're earning it working for me. There'll be no debt." Cade said, concentrating on the traffic.

He glanced in the rear view mirror—the little boy was asleep, tilted sideways in the car seat.

Caleb. How could any man father such an adorable child and not want to acknowledge him? Maybe he'd see what he could do to locate the man. See the happiness in Jordan's eyes again.

Of course, Caleb's father didn't know of his existence.

Once again, Cade tried to picture someone using his name. It sounded like someone that knew him and the ranch, from what Jordan had said. Yet he couldn't come up with anyone he knew with blond hair and blue eyes who was the right age to be Caleb's father.

Jordan was resting her head on the back of the seat. Had she fallen asleep, too?

When she stirred, he took the chance she was awake.

"Tell me more about Caleb's father. I'm still trying to figure out who would have used my name."

"I've told you all I remember. He was so much fun, swept me off my feet. He was tall and athletic. He could swim like a fish and loved to body surf. He wore sunglasses a lot, maybe to hide his eyes, but I didn't think so at the time. They were as blue as Caleb's."

"He was blond, you said."

"Yes. About six feet two. He had a high opinion of himself—which I shared until he left."

"What did you do after that?"

It wasn't like him to ask so many questions of strangers. She'd work for him until Penny came back, then return to Florida. They would not remain in contact once she left. Yet he wanted to know more about her, know everything that happened to her. Try to get a handle on the woman who had overcome such hardships and come out with such an optimistic view of life.

"I finished high school before I realized I was pregnant. College was out of the question once I decided to keep Caleb. Aunt Maggie helped, and I went full time at Joe's Taco Shack."

"What did you want to study in college?"

She looked at him a moment, as if weighing his reaction to her reply.

"Architecture."

That startled him.

"Shopping malls and office complexes?"

"No, family homes. I've never lived in one and thought it would be so great to design homes for families of all sizes. There's such a wide variety of architectural styles for houses, from very modern, to reproductions of Victorian, to old-fashioned farmhouses. Depending on the building lot and the lifestyle of the people who would live in it, I thought I could design the perfect home for each customer."

"You could still go to college and get that degree."

"Maybe, once Caleb's in school. In the meantime, I have enough to do with Caleb and work."

He wondered how she managed on a waitress' salary. It had to be difficult, yet she had never even hinted he might help her out financially. Was that coming later? Would she find reasons to stay in Texas, reasons to try to get him to finance her new lifestyle?

He doubted it. It might be easier if she did.

Dinner with everyone at the table that evening was more relaxed than the night before. Cade was tired—not having slept for two days was making its impact. He ate Rosita's delicious cooking, trying to distance himself from the others at the table. But despite his best efforts, he was intrigued with Jordan Carhart.

Her eyes sparkled when she told Amelia about the Friday surgery date. She laughed at something Caleb said, her cheeks flushed with warmth, her eyes full of love.

He wanted to touch that soft hair, brush it back from her face and cradle her head in his hands, holding her for a kiss, not cut and run like a scared rabbit.

But a kiss that would make him forget the past and open the door to something new. It had been a long time since he'd kissed anyone, but he wanted Jordan.

"I'll go with you to the hospital on Friday," Amelia said.

"You don't have to do that. We have to be there at six in the morning. I figured I'd have to leave around 4:30 am. to make it on time," Jordan said.

"You'll want someone with you while you're waiting. I'm not so old I can't get up early once in a while, young lady."

"Thank you, Amelia. I'll be grateful for your support."

Amelia looked at Cade. "Will you be going with us?"

Cade shook his head, catching the disappointed look on Caleb's face. "Tomorrow and Friday, I'll be out with the cattle. We've delayed moving the major portion of the herd as it is because of the late rain and the muddy fields."

"The men can handle it," Amelia said primly. "You should be with us."

Cade hated hospitals. Hadn't he heard the worst news of his life in one? Even the thought of entering another had him tensing. Jordan didn't need him. If she'd stayed in Florida, when the operation had come, she'd have been alone.

He didn't like the thought.

"We'll manage fine. I couldn't ask Cade to skip a day of work for us. It's bad enough I'm missing a day when I just started," Jordan said firmly. "We'll drive in early and have breakfast there once Caleb's settled."

Cade had visions of her old car breaking down in the predawn morning, stalling on the highway, of someone not seeing it and slamming into it in the dark.

"Take my car," he said abruptly.

"What?"

"It'll be more reliable than yours."

Jordan bristled. "My car is perfectly fine, thank you very much."

Cade said nothing, but he'd make sure she took a more reliable vehicle than that old beater of hers. He couldn't dispel the image of a fiery crash.

After dinner, Jordan bathed Caleb and talked to him about the upcoming surgery. The doctor had given them a little book designed to explain things to young children. She was getting ready to tuck him into bed when Cade appeared.

"Hi Mr. Everett," Caleb called from his bed. "Did you come to tuck me in, too?"

For a moment Cade relived the bedtime ritual he'd had with Vicki. Both he and Marissa tried to be with her when time for bed, reading her a story, talking about her day, and tucking her into bed.

The little boy looked hopeful as he smiled at Cade.

"I came to talk to your mother when she's finished here," he said gruffly.

"Oh."

The disappointment was almost tangible.

"But now that Cade's here, he can help me tuck you in, can't you?"

Jordan's glare clearly conveyed her message—help or else.

Cade stepped inside and crossed to the bed.

"Good night," he said.

"You have to tuck in the covers," Caleb said.

Cade pulled the covers taut, tucking them around Caleb.

"Sleep well," he said, stepping back.

Jordan kissed her son and hugged him.

"Tomorrow you can tell Mr. Murray all about your operation."

"And about getting ice cream when I'm good for the operation," Caleb added.

"That's right. I love you, Caleb," she said, kissing him again.

"Night Mommy. Night Mr. Everett."

"Call me Cade," Cade said.

Might as well. The longer name was a mouthful for a little kid.

When they closed the door to the room behind them, Jordan turned.

"What did you want to see me about?" she asked.

He was too close. She could feel the heat of his body envelop her. Was he deliberately invading her space? Slowly, she took a step backward to a safer distance. She almost laughed. He hadn't kissed her last night, and she doubted he had any plans in that direction tonight. She was letting her imagination take flight.

He didn't seem to be aware of her discomfort or crazy thoughts. Not about the kiss and not about the fact she wanted to fling herself into his arms and have him tell her everything would be all right.

No one could guarantee that. And he'd probably think her certifiably crazy if she did so.

"I wanted to discuss a few things about work. How about we go out on the veranda? The evening's still warm," he suggested.

She nodded, her heart skipping a beat. It had been on the veranda he'd almost kissed her. Hadn't he?

Not that she would encourage that kind of thing, even if he were interested.

Jordan knew her stay was temporary. She had no more illusions about love and marriage and happily ever after. She'd thought she was in love with the boy she'd met at spring break, but as time had passed, she realized she'd been in love with the illusion of love. With the fantasy of devotion and fun and desire. They had little in common—like honesty and reliability. She knew so little about the man who had fathered Caleb.

She'd grown since then. Now she felt more mature and more discerning. She wanted a lot more than a casual fling, no matter how appealing it might be with Cade.

He gestured toward the rockers to the right of the front door, and Jordan sat in one. She had a view of the rolling hills, fading to black as the night came down.

She could hear the murmur of voices from the bunkhouse. Once in a while a man laughed.

Cade sat in the chair beside her, where he'd been last night when she'd found him.

"I'll be going up with the herd tomorrow, and we won't be back until late. If Stevenson calls, refer him to Hank in the Dallas office. I don't expect any major problems, but if they arise, I'll carry my cell phone. Call if there's an emergency."

"Otherwise, I'll tell everyone you'll call them back on Monday?"

"I'll be back in the late afternoon. Still time to call LA if needed. But handle what you can yourself. Activate the answering machine at the end of the day. It can take messages Friday."

"Me field your calls? I know nothing about what you're doing. I'm lucky not to disconnect callers any more."

"You pick up things faster than the two temps from the agency in town did."

Jordan felt a warm glow at his halfhearted compliment. She'd been doing her best in an alien environment. It was nothing like waiting tables. She was happy to hear it wasn't all in vain.

"About Friday," Cade began.

"My car will work," she said stubbornly.

"My car would be more comfortable for Aunt Amelia," he replied quickly.

She looked at him in the growing darkness. She hadn't considered Amelia. Was she letting foolish pride stand in her way? The older woman was coming to help her out. Maybe she should take his blasted car and stop arguing.

"I hadn't thought about that," she murmured.

"Think about it."

"It's bigger than what I'm used to."

"I could have one of the men drive you in. But I need them for the cattle. When will you be ready to return?"

"I don't know. After Caleb goes to sleep, I guess. Do you think Amelia would stay that long? Maybe she shouldn't go with us after all. It could be a long day. I can get a hotel room nearby."

"She wants to go. Let her. She'll talk your ear off and make you forget your worries for a while. And I'm the last one to suggest she'll get tired. She'd set me in my place fast."

"Does she do that to you?" Jordan asked softly, trying to imagine his delicate aunt talking endlessly and Cade just sitting and listening.

"Talk my ear off? Sometimes."

"I bet she tells you wonderful stories about Vicki," she said slowly.

"We don't talk about Vicki around here," he said heavily.

"Why ever not? I'd want to talk about Caleb all the time, to make sure everyone remembered him. To celebrate his life. To remember the great times together."

Jordan had heard Amelia when she mentioned Cade never talked about Vicki, but she didn't understand it.

"Memories can be painful," Cade said slowly.

"Yes. I know because I've really missed Aunt Maggie since she died. But now I can laugh at some memories of things we did. I always feel a poignant longing to go back to the way things were when Caleb was an infant, or even before when it was just Aunt Maggie and me. But I know I can't. So I do what I can to celebrate her life. She was so special to me. She raised me after my folks died. That couldn't have been easy. She never married, was in her fifties when I came to live with her. Yet she loved me and later Caleb like we were always her own."

Impulsively, Jordan reached out and grabbed Cade's hand.

"Tell me one special memory you have of Vicki."

Her aunt was the one who always *did*. Maybe Cade needed to do something, even if only to recall one special event in his daughter's life.

His fingers tightened on hers, but he remained silent for a long time. Finally, he began to speak.

"The first time I took her up with me on a horse. We rode to the river and back. She held on to the reins, and I let her think she was directing the horse. She laughed and yelled and slapped those reins on the horse's neck. Her soft baby hair blew up into my face. Marissa didn't cut it until she started school, so at age three it was long and fine and smelled like baby girl. She laughed the entire way, delighting in being up on an enormous horse with her daddy."

Jordan could envision the happiness the day must have held. She knew the little girl had lacked for nothing in this family. Love spilled out with every word Cade said. She wished for a moment Cade had been Caleb's father. What a wonderful father he must have been.

"Tell me all about her. What color was her hair? Did she like vegetables? What was her favorite song?" Jordan urged.

Slowly at first, then more easily, he opened up. For two

hours, Cade talked about his little girl. Marissa figured prominently in many of the scenarios he recounted, and Jordan drew a mental image of the close-knit, loving family. How doubly tragic it all ended so soon.

When Cade stopped, she realized he still held her hand. She had never felt closer to another person, except Aunt Maggie, than she did with Cade Everett at this moment.

The night was quiet around them. The air had cooled down, but it was still pleasantly comfortable. The stars were brilliant points of glittering light in the black velvet sky.

Not wanting to break the mood, Jordan didn't know how to leave. She felt as if she'd been given a precious gift, made even more special coming from Cade.

He solved her problem.

"I'm tired. I'd better head for bed. We leave at first light in the morning."

His voice was gruff.

"Thanks for telling me about Vicki," she whispered, rising when he did.

He released her hand, but caught her shoulders in a light hold.

"You're a dangerous woman, Jordan Carhart. I haven't talked about Vicki since her death. I had almost forgotten all those special times."

"But didn't you have fun tonight remembering how special she was? I know it hurts to have her gone, but you have such wonderful memories. I believe she was truly a happy child her entire life."

"You've given me the gift of my daughter again. Thank you."

He drew her closer and kissed her.

Jordan wasn't prepared for a kiss. The sensations that swept through her caught her unaware, then flared into bright heat. His mouth was warm and enticing. The kiss was the most exciting thing she'd ever experienced. When he parted her lips with his tongue, she felt a warmth wash through her hotter than the Texas sun. Her legs felt weak, and she hoped she wouldn't melt into a puddle at his feet. Twining her arms around his neck, she gave back as good as she got, relishing every heartbeat, every inch of his body pressed against hers. She savored the feel of her soft body against his harder one. She had never felt such a connection, such a feeling of wonder and rightness.

He deepened the kiss, and she forgot about gratitude and lost children and feeling alive, and relished every magical moment when her life seemed to spin to the heavens.

He kissed her as no man ever had, and she delighted in every stolen moment.

When he slowly eased back, she felt bereft. She didn't want to stop. They could have kissed all night, and it'd end too soon.

But he was her boss. The man who was helping her with her son's expenses for the operation, not someone to fantasize about.

A kiss to thank her for rekindling memories, that was all.

She'd do best to keep that firmly in mind. A man's attention wouldn't fool her a second time. She had her life charted, and side trips into sexual fantasy weren't on the map.

"I'll take good care of the office tomorrow," she said breathlessly, then turned and fled for the safety of her room.

She was getting in over her head with Cade Everett. Hadn't she learned from her prior experience? This was not some courtship leading to happily ever after. At least the man she'd known in South Beach had pretended Cade had never given her a morsel of hope. She had better remember that every moment she remained on the Everett ranch.

Jordan found the office flat with Cade gone. As part of her duties, she fielded telephone calls, received emailed reports which she promptly printed and placed on his desk, and completed the filing. She was proud he'd left her to her own devices. She wasn't the office assistant he was used to, but she was coping.

Caleb came to see her shortly before lunch and she let him play on the computer until she took her lunch break.

The afternoon seemed to drag. She read some reports that had come in, but they confused her. She didn't understand all that was going on, but she knew Cade was a key player in several large corporations, as well as the boss of the family ranch.

Just before Jordan was about to call it a day and close up, a flashy red sports utility vehicle drove up and parked right in front of the office. A tall, slim young woman exited, glanced around, and headed into the office.

Her dark hair spilled down in a glossy waterfall across her shoulders. Her makeup was flawless. Her shirt looked tailored and her designer jeans looked brand new, topping polished snake skin boots.

Jordan was instantly aware of the differences between the two of them—her off the rack jeans and shirt, no makeup and who knew what her hair looked like.

"Cade around?" she drawled, eyeing Jordan like she was an alien.

"He's out on the range today," Jordan said politely.

She knew how to deal with the public—even people she didn't like. And this person was definitely not destined to become her best friend.

"I can tell Cade you stopped by, shall I, Miss?"

"Gloria Devon."

She wandered to the door of Cade's office and looked in.

Jordan wondered if Gloria didn't believe her and was checking for herself. Did she and Cade have a friendship that allowed her to wander into his office? Not knowing, Jordan would rather err on the side of caution. She rose and moved swiftly to the door beside Gloria. As far as Jordan knew, Gloria had no business going into Cade's private office and if she stepped one foot inside—

Gloria turned and walked back to Jordan's desk, sitting carelessly on one corner and studying Jordan.

"I heard from Amelia that Cade had someone taking Penny's place until she returns. I live on the adjacent ranch. Cade and I are close friends. Very close friends. Have you heard when Penny's coming back?"

Jordan blinked, feeling a twinge of jealousy. Cade had kissed her last night, but was close with this woman? Of course their kiss had meant nothing. Why would he ever look at her when he had a relationship with this beauty?

Even more reason to keep a tight rein on her emotions. The lecture she'd given herself last night rose, and she reminded herself to repeat it at every opportunity.

Cade Everett was not for her.

"I haven't spoken with Penny. I don't know what she's told Cade," Jordan said, feeling at a loss. Despite everything, she loved the kiss, and woven fantasies around it.

Now they vanished as in a puff of smoke. Once again, reality was staring her in the face.

"I could have helped Cade around here. He should have asked me," Gloria said, glancing around the office. "Let him know I'm available, will you?"

Jordan wisely kept silent. She wouldn't be drawn into a discussion with this stranger over the actions of her boss. Her loyalty lay with Cade. And she couldn't help thinking once he knew Gloria was available, her time as office assistant would be limited.

Gloria stood and glanced around once more, as if trying to discover something that would keep her longer. Finding nothing, she shrugged.

"Tell Cade to call me. There's a barbecue tomorrow night at Ted Sampson's place. I thought Cade could take me."

"I don't think so," Cade replied from the doorway.

Jordan leaned to one side so she could see around Gloria. He walked in, slapping a dusty hat against equally dusty jeans. He looked hard, tired, dirty—and wonderful.

Jordan didn't know if she was up to watching Gloria and Cade interact, not that she had any choice in the matter. How did such close friends greet each other—with no holds barred, or more discretely?

"Hi, Cade." Gloria greeted him enthusiastically, going

over as if to give him a hug.

He stepped back, holding up his hand.

"I'm dusty and sweaty. What are you doing here, Gloria?"

"Like I was telling your new little secretary, Ted is throwing a barbecue tomorrow night. I'm sure you got an invitation. Since we live so close, I thought we could go over together. That way, I wouldn't have to worry about driving back home all by my lonesome after dark."

Her flirtatious look spoke volumes.

Oh, please, Jordan thought. Anyone more capable she'd never seen. She suspected Gloria never gave a thought to driving anywhere by herself, no matter what the time of day or night. Why not come out and tell the man she wanted him to take her because of their involvement? Or were they keeping it a secret for some reason? Whatever, Jordan didn't want to stand and watch.

"Isn't your father going?" Cade asked.

"No, he's in El Paso, won't be home until next week sometime. Come on, Cade. It'll be fun to see all your neighbors and enjoy yourself a bit. You are such a hermit these days."

Jordan waited for him to blast her for treading on sensitive turf, but he merely shook his head.

"No can do, Gloria. I already have plans."

"What plans?"

"I'm taking Jordan to Dallas tomorrow. Her son's having surgery and I need to be there."

Chapter Six

Jordan almost dropped her jaw. Cade was telling Gloria he needed to be with her when Caleb had his surgery? She was stunned. Though not as surprised as Gloria seemed when she spun around to glare at Jordan.

"You're going to the hospital with her? She has a child and you're involved? What happened to your famous vow to stay away from entanglements and from all children?" she asked, hands on hips, glaring at Cade.

Jordan felt a small spurt of pleasure to see the anger on the woman's face. She studied Cade. He didn't seem very perturbed to have Gloria angry at him.

"I've been waiting for two years for you to loosen up a little. Here's a perfect opportunity to get back in the swing of things, and you're going to some hospital with a stranger?" Gloria almost shouted.

"I don't know what you mean about waiting, but I'm driving Jordan in tomorrow morning early and I don't know when we'll be back, but not tomorrow night. We're staying in a hotel in town close to the hospital," Cade said, his eyes narrowed as he regarded his neighbor warily.

If looks could injure, Gloria's venomous expression

would have shriveled Jordan right up.

She wanted to protest she knew nothing about Cade's plans, but loyalty kept her quiet. And curious.

What was he doing telling her such a tall tale? Amelia was going with her. Granted, they'd discussed staying at the hotel closest to the hospital together, but no mention of Cade had been made. Jordan thought he was needed with the cattle roundup or something.

"Call me when you finish playing nursemaid," Gloria said, stalking out.

They heard the car door slam. When the wheels spun and squealed, Jordan dared a glance at Cade. He was watching her.

"She has a bit of a temper," he said.

Wisely, Jordan decided not to respond to that.

"I didn't expect you back until later."

"My horse threw a shoe. We didn't have a replacement with us, so I brought him in to have it fixed."

She purposely didn't bring up his startling comment he was going into Dallas with her, but she wanted to. Would he? Or was that just an excuse for the pushy Gloria? What exactly was their relationship? Not that it mattered, Jordan tried to convince herself. She and Cade were not involved.

"Anything crucial? Or do I have time to go get cleaned up before dinner?" he asked.

"There were two phone calls I referred to the Dallas office. The rest said they could wait until Monday. Hank sent you a long report that I printed, and you got two others that were single sheets."

She couldn't contain her curiosity any longer.

"Did you mean it when you said you're driving us into Dallas, or was that just an excuse for Gloria?"

"I meant it."

He turned and headed toward the house to shower and change before dinner.

Jordan watched him walk away. Had something happened she didn't know about? Why was he involving himself in her problem after saying he wanted to keep his distance?

Amelia said he never took part in family events anymore. Why would he do something for her—a stranger?

Gloria had been right. From what had happened to his family, helping Jordan out seemed to be the last thing he'd want to do. Yet she was sure she'd just heard him say he was accompanying them tomorrow.

Amelia was as surprised as Jordan to learn of Cade's change of plans. She'd reserved a suite at the hotel closest to the hospital, thinking she and Jordan would need some time and space to be rested for Caleb.

If Cade accompanied them, they'd have to share the suite—or he'd have to get his own room. She watched Cade throughout dinner, trying to divine what had happened to the man. He appeared unconcerned, but Amelia knew something was up. He hadn't been interested in anything except work for months.

Speculatively, she glanced at Jordan and then Caleb, then back to her nephew.

Immediately following their evening meal, Cade left for the office, with strict instructions for everyone to get to bed early. They'd leave promptly at 4:30 in the morning.

Since Caleb would don a hospital gown once they arrived, Jordan let him wear his pajamas the next morning for the ride into the city.

The air was crisp and cool, the stars still brilliant in the sky, dawn more than an hour away as they pulled away from the house.

Jordan felt keyed up, apprehensive, and still amazed the operation was actually going to take place. Even when she paid Cade back the money, she'd never be able to repay his kindness to a stranger.

Cade drove swiftly through the dark, saying little, listening to his aunt. Amelia sat in the front with him, sipping coffee Rosita had prepared and chatting almost nonstop. Jordan tried to relax, but she was edgy and nervous. Her precious little boy was having surgery.

All thanks to the man driving. A complex creature whom she'd never have suspected of warmth from their first encounter. Yet who was single-handedly doing more for her son than anyone else ever had.

Once again, she wished he had been Caleb's father. Not that Cade would have acted like Caleb's biological father had, but a woman could dream.

Once they arrived at the hospital, he handled everything efficiently and with no wasted energy. Before Jordan realized it, Caleb had been wheeled away, and she was left in the surgery waiting room with Cade and Amelia—with four hours ahead before Caleb would be in recovery.

Restless, she paced the small waiting room, praying Caleb's good spirits would hold, that the operation would be a success, that nothing would go wrong.

"Let's go for breakfast," Cade suggested, glancing around. "This place makes me edgy."

"I couldn't eat anything," Jordan replied.

"I could. And you need to. He'll be raring to go when he's out of here. You're already too thin. You need to put some pounds on," Cade said.

"He's right, dear. We'll need all our energy when he's home. I think a nice breakfast will help in more ways than one. We can't just keep our eye on the clock. Time would pass too slowly," Amelia said, adding her weight to the argument.

Outnumbered, Jordan nodded.

"But only as far as the hospital cafeteria. I'll leave word at the nurses' station."

While the cafeteria wasn't crowded—it was too early— there were still several people ahead of them. Jordan had an omelet made to order. Amelia wandered to the cereal display. Cade came up behind Jordan, watching the short-order cook as he scrambled eggs, fried them and kept a steady stream of bacon and sausages cooking.

"Why did you change your mind and decide to come today?" she asked, glancing up at him. "Was it something Gloria said?"

"No, I decided before seeing her. I began thinking yesterday on the ride back to the house what I'd want someone to do for Vicki had the circumstances been different. I don't know who used my name five years ago, but it tied us together."

He hesitated a moment, as if gearing up for a hard

confession, then continued, "I'll never get to see my daughter grow up, get married, provide me with grandchildren. But I used to like kids. Still do, I guess. I've shut myself away from them lately. Marissa and Vicki both would be disappointed. Maybe helping Caleb can show them I haven't abdicated life's responsibilities because they are no longer here with me."

"You're a kind man, Cade. Anyone else would have shut the door in my face or cried fraud or something that first afternoon," Jordan said.

She hated feeling so beholden, but would do almost anything for her son. She just hoped in her life, she could pass on the kindness.

He glanced around, then leaned close, almost whispering in her ear.

"I have a reputation in this town. Don't you dare repeat you think I'm kind."

Jordan laughed, as she suspected was his intent. His dark eyes gazed down into hers. For a moment she longed to step into his arms, rest in the safety they offered. She yearned to feel his mouth on hers again, to lean against his strength. She wished she had that right with an intensity that frightened her.

But, as Aunt Maggie always said, that which doesn't harm us strengthens us. Jordan had been on her own for years. Nothing had changed since meeting Cade. She deliberately stepped away from temptation.

She had to be strong for her son. It was the two of them against the world. This time with Cade was magical, but fleeting. Soon they'd be on their way back to Florida, with memories to last a lifetime. And a debt she could never fully repay.

Less than an hour passed before they returned to the

surgery waiting room. Cade hesitated in the doorway, then looked at Jordan.

"Amelia will stay with you. I can't stay here. I'm going into work. Here's my cell number. Let me know as soon as you hear something."

"Okay." Jordan put the number into her phone, disappointed he wasn't staying, but trying not to show it. He'd already given her more time than she had a right to expect.

Once he left, she sat beside Amelia.

"I expect it was hard for him to be here, don't you think?" she asked the older woman, feeling anxiety creep in. She prayed her son would be all right.

"He had to go to the hospital when he was called about Marissa and Vicki—to identify them. I don't expect any experience with such a facility will ever be easy in the future. It will always hold memories of that horrible day," Amelia said.

Jordan nodded. It made his coming and staying as long as he did even more special. She just couldn't help wishing he'd stayed a little longer.

The rest of the morning seemed to drag by in a blur. She and Amelia talked desultorily. She leafed through magazines, paced to the window, and tried not to watch the clock.

Finally, the surgeon came out to report on the success of the operation. Jordan was allowed into the children's recovery room to await Caleb's return to consciousness. He had bandages over his left eye and looked so small and pale in the big bed her heart turned over.

She dialed Cade.

He answered on the first ring.

"Hi, it's me. Caleb's out of surgery. Every thing went well."

Jordan burst into tears.

"Jordan?"

She tried to stop the tears, but the relief was so overwhelming, she couldn't.

"Tell me," he ordered.

"Everything is fine," she repeated, trying to speak coherently.

What a ninny. She should have waited to call him, or at least waited to fall apart.

"I'll be right there."

He disconnected before she could protest.

A nurse stopped in, saw Jordan and came to check on her, rubbing her shoulder compassionately when she learned of the reason for the tears.

"It's hard when they're kids, isn't it?" she said, offering a tissue. "But he's going to be fine and better than before. Dr. Tamsin has a well-deserved reputation for doing outstanding work. Caleb won't wake up for a while, and when he finally does, he'll be groggy and ready to go back to sleep almost immediately. You have time to go for a cup of tea if you like."

Jordan shook her head.

"I'll wait here. Sorry to be a bother."

"No bother. He's a lucky boy to have a doting mother."

The nurse patted her on the shoulder again, checked Caleb's vital signs and moved on to the second occupied bed in the recovery room.

Jordan bunched up the tissue and watched her son sleep. He was going to be fine, his eyes fixed and able to track like everyone else. She was so relieved the ordeal was over.

Ten minutes later, Cade strode into the Recovery Room, heading straight for Jordan. She looked up, surprised.

"Cade, what are you doing here?"

He leaned over her.

"Are you all right? Is Caleb all right?"

She nodded, feeling the tears well in her eyes.

"I came as soon as I could. Traffic was a bear."

He studied her for a moment, then looked at Caleb.

"If he's going to be okay, why the tears? Was there a complication, after all?"

"No, it was just the relief," she said, trying to staunch the new flow of tears with the bunched up tissue.

Cade had left work to come because he thought she needed him. The knowledge overwhelmed her. No one had ever done that for her before. Tears were the only way to relieve the tension that filled her.

"Here." he thrust a clean handkerchief into her hand.

As she blotted her eyes, he pulled her to her feet and wrapped his arms around her. Jordan had never felt so safe. She leaned slightly against him, relishing his arms holding her, the steady, comforting beat of his heart beneath her ear, the feeling that life would go on and she would make it.

All from being held in his embrace.

How lucky Marissa had been to have such a wonderful man for her husband. For a long moment, she drew strength from him. Then Jordan drew a shaky breath and stepped back, breaking his hold. She couldn't allow her boss to hold her. It wasn't right.

Not only that, she was enjoying it too much. She needed to keep some distance between them. He had done so much for them. She didn't want him to think she expected anything further.

She had to remind herself she worked for him. Temporarily. When Penny returned, Jordan would be on her way back to Florida before she could say order-up.

The thought was depressing, but she clung to it and put some distance between them.

"Thank you for coming. I really am a silly goose to be so teary when the news is good. But it's such a relief," she said.

Cade gestured to the chair, and Jordan sat. He perched on the arm and asked what she'd been told about Caleb's recovery.

When learning that once Caleb recovered from the anesthetic he'd still be groggy and most likely go right back to sleep, Cade insisted she go to the hotel later to get a good night's rest.

"I wanted to stay here."

"He'll be asleep, Jordan. He won't even know if you're here or not. We'll be less than five minutes away and can come in an instant if there is a need. But if he sleeps through the night, it'll give you time to sleep as well. You'll want to be rested for tomorrow."

She studied her son as Cade studied her. It was only early afternoon, yet she already looked tired. She needed rest to keep her energy up. And to eat more. Had she and Amelia had lunch?

He rose, intent on finding his aunt and making sure she

took care of Jordan.

She drew her gaze from Caleb to look at him.

"Are you leaving?"

"Do you want me to stay?"

Hesitating, she shook her head.

"No, I'm fine. There's nothing you can do."

He knew that. But for an instant, he wished there was something he could do to help. To shelter her from the trials and tribulations of life. He didn't want to analyze that protective streak too closely.

The thought surprised him. He didn't normally go into a protective mode for other people. Jordan lived her entire life until a couple of weeks ago without his help. She'd do fine without it in the future.

He was growing too involved with her and her son.

Losing Marissa and Vicki had been almost more than one man could stand. He refused to put his emotions on the line a second time. Getting involved with women, and especially children, was risky. Getting involved with this woman wasn't in the cards. She'd come looking for someone else. She was still searching for the man she'd loved enough to make a child with. He wasn't that man.

And he couldn't offer any woman what she'd want—a devoted husband, father to her children, a future. The risk of further heartache was too great. Once in a lifetime was all he could endure.

"I'll check with Aunt Amelia and return to work. Call me if you need me."

She nodded and tried to smile.

"Thanks for coming over. Sorry to interrupt whatever you were doing."

Jordan watched as Cade left the large recovery room. He looked so fit striding across the floor, one nurse stepping out of his way and then turning to watch. He looked neither to the right nor left. Probably couldn't wait to get out of the hospital.

But her heart warmed at the reality of his coming. He'd thought she needed him and he came at once.

Such a contrast to the man she'd thought she'd loved so many years ago. He'd vanished without a trace—after leaving a string of lies. She had been gullible, as Aunt Maggie had said. She was wiser now. And almost regretted the fact.

Cade would never lie. A woman would know exactly where she stood with him. As Jordan did. He'd helped Caleb because he could no longer help his own daughter. But there was no tie beyond that. No matter how much she might wish there were.

Amelia insisted Jordan take breaks from sitting by the bed of the sleeping child. When they moved Caleb to the Pediatrics Floor, Jordan went for a quick walk around the hospital grounds. The fresh air felt good, but it was a quick break. She wanted to be at his side when Caleb awoke.

It was after seven when Jordan agreed to leave with Amelia. Caleb had been awake, eaten a light meal, and drifted back to sleep. The nurse on duty had told Jordan she expected Caleb to sleep all night. The drip from the IV would keep him hydrated, nourished and pain free, so there was no reason for him to waken before morning.

Agreeing to call if he did, she shooed Jordan and Amelia away from his bed.

They took a cab to the hotel, Jordan feeling wrung out and cranky.

"We'll order room service, I think," Amelia said as they rode up in the elevator. "A quick shower will revive you long enough to eat. I know you're tired, but you need to eat, as well as sleep. Actually, once we finish dinner, it'll be bed for both of us. I'm not used to getting up so early and then spending the day away from home. I didn't even have time to nap."

"Oh, Amelia, you shouldn't have stayed all day," Jordan said, feeling guilty.

The elevator stopped on their floor, and the elderly lady headed for their suite.

"Nonsense. I love that boy, too, you know. I had to be near in case. Rosita and I are looking forward to taking care of him while he recovers. No strenuous exercise for six weeks, the doctor said. We've got cards and board games and videos lined up. She asked her grandchildren what they liked the best, so we have exactly what will appeal to a boy at that age. But it's a surprise, something new for each day, so don't be telling him anything."

"He'll love it. Thank you."

Jordan gave her an impulsive hug. Where would she be without these people helping her? It was so unexpected she still felt she was dreaming.

Cade was on the phone in the sitting room of the suite when they entered. He quickly ended the call and rose to greet Amelia and Jordan. He studied Jordan closely, then seemed satisfied.

"Did you two eat?" he asked.

"We wanted room service," Amelia said. "Did you eat?"

"No, I called the hospital just as you two were leaving, so I waited."

The service was quick and before long, the three of them shared a meal in front of the large window that overlooked Dallas. The lights shining from the buildings and dwellings coupled with the streetlights gave a fairy tale glow to the land. When she had finished dinner, Amelia excused herself and headed for bed.

"Are you too tired to stay up a little longer?" Cade asked Jordan.

"No, I'm still keyed up from today's events. I still can't believe the operation I've saved for, for so long is over. Of course, this only means the beginning of more treatment and therapy, but according to the doctor, within a few months, both eyes will track together. We owe it all to you."

"You would have managed, just taken a little longer," he murmured.

"I wish I could repay you, beyond the money, I mean. You don't know how grateful I am."

"I'm not after gratitude," he growled.

Jordan fell silent. What was he after? As far as she could tell, Cade went through the motions of living, but a part of him had died with Marissa and Vicki.

She understood it. She thought life had ended when her Cade Cullen Everett had disappeared. But she'd had a baby to care for, and gradually life had regained its glow. Until Aunt Maggie died.

One of the hardest aspects of death was the fact those

surviving had to move on. Life continued. And it never came with any guarantees it wouldn't try to crush you beneath its blows.

Jordan hadn't been crushed, though it seemed like it at the time. She wished she could show him life still had much to offer.

Cade stared at Jordan. He saw color rise in her cheeks, and her eyes dart toward his, then away, as if afraid to meet his gaze lest she see something in it she didn't want to see.

And that would be what, he thought heavily. Lust?

When she said she was grateful, anger flared. That was not something he wanted. He'd kissed her, tasted the sweetness of her mouth. And he wanted more.

For the first time in years, his libido sprang to life at the thought of someone beside Marissa. He wanted Jordan Carhart.

Emotions churning, he pushed back his chair and walked to the window. Leaning against the sill with both hands, he stared sightlessly out into the dark. The lights twinkling gave no delight. He was looking inward and hated what he saw.

Desire for a woman beside his wife. It didn't matter that Marissa had been dead for two years. It felt like a betrayal. Betrayal of her, of his vow to remain uninvolved. Betrayal of the trust Jordan had placed in him. Damn, he could control it. He would. Taking a deep breath, he almost jumped when she touched his arm. He hadn't heard her move to cross the room.

Slowly, he straightened and turned toward her. The lighting seemed bright after the darkness of the night. He narrowed his gaze against it, taking in the uncertainty of her expression, the soft swell of her breasts, the fragrance that whispered Jordan, Jordan, Jordan.

Without thinking, he drew her into his arms and lowered his head. The first touch of her lips drove all thoughts from his mind. Guilt fled. Desire sparked. This felt too right to be wrong.

Marissa was gone. Jordan was here. Alive, warm, sweet and so sexy it drove him crazy.

She held nothing back as he deepened the kiss. His tongue touched hers, mated, swept through her mouth as if he would devour her. Heat rose between them, and he could feel her breasts press against his chest, feel them swell with desire. Her arms wound around his neck and she held on as if she'd never let him go.

One kiss would never be enough. He wanted her as a man wants a woman, completely, totally. He rubbed his hands down her back, lifting her closer, nestling against her as if he'd sought comfort or more.

Every breath was filled with her scent. Every heartbeat increased his body heat until he felt he would ignite. His mouth against hers only had him longing to touch other parts of her. He moved to kiss her cheeks, trail short nibbles along her jaw, down to the rapidly beating pulse point at the base of her throat. When he licked it, her skin was pure ambrosia. She moaned softly in her throat and he felt as if he could capture the sound with his lips.

He brushed back the collar of her blouse and tasted the softness of her shoulders. He felt her own mouth move against his ear, along his cheek, back to his lips.

Mindful of Aunt Amelia only a few steps away, he knew they couldn't go anywhere with this—even if Jordan would agree.

Slowly, reality returned. He kissed her mouth gently one last time and eased her away, gazing down into her slightly blurred eyes.

She blinked slowly and met his gaze as confusion and desire mingled.

"If that was because you're grateful, I'll put my fist through the wall," he murmured.

She shook her head.

"I might be grateful, but for that, I'd just say thank you."

She reached out and trailed her fingers down his cheek, rubbed against the evening beard along his jaw as if mesmerized by the texture, by the slight rasping sound. Her eyes followed her fingertips for a moment, then met his gaze once again.

"Why did you kiss me?" she asked softly.

"Because I want you."

At her startled look, he almost smiled. She had to have known from the level of the kiss there was more than just a brush of lips.

"Been there, done that. It sure didn't turn out the way I thought it would," she said flippantly.

She was flat-out scared. She'd thought she had loved the man she knew as Cade Cullen Everett, but that proved false. Now she didn't trust her senses, her own mind or heart. She could fall for this man and end up the same way—alone with a boatload of regrets.

Backing away, she looked so sad Cade wanted to grab her up in another embrace and kiss her until she couldn't think of anything or anyone else. Make her forget the past.

But she obviously remembered another time. Another man. Could he blame her for being wary? Especially when all he wanted was time with her, a few hours, days. Not a future, not forever.

"Go to bed, Jordan. Tomorrow you'll have your hands full with Caleb."

The swiftness of her departure would have hurt a weaker man, he thought cynically. But he suspected she was the wiser of the two of them.

Chapter Seven

A week later, Jordan had almost forgotten the kiss. At least that was what she told herself endless times during the day whenever the memory of that night arose.

The first few days Caleb was home from the hospital were hectic. Mindful of her obligation, she took an hour or two each day to check the mail. The office phone was switched to ring in the house and she took messages from there. Cade spent the week in Dallas, not even returning home in the evenings.

She wondered if he deliberately stayed away, but found it unlikely. He did what he wanted and wouldn't have been upset by her flight that night. She was the one who wished she'd handled things differently, with more sophistication.

She'd been a wildly willing participant in that kiss. Why wouldn't he think she'd be open to more? Especially considering what he knew of her history.

But the defection of Caleb's father had hurt her too much. She was a coward, totally afraid to risk her heart again. Especially with a man who had buried his own heart with his wife and child.

Jordan finally put in a full day in the office, filing letters and reports, answering the phone, receiving reports from Cade's far-flung empire. She was growing adept at office work and liked it. Maybe she'd try for a desk job when she returned to Florida instead of working at the Shack.

Just before four, she heard a familiar engine in the driveway. She rose and hurried to the window in anticipation. Cade had returned. Jordan watched as he walked into the house, with not even a glance toward the office.

She sighed softly, knowing her decision to flee the other night had been wise, but wishing things were different. Wishing she could make Cade remember what it was to embrace life to the fullest, to enjoy the companionship of another, to plan for a future together. To love.

She blinked and drew in a sharp breath.

She was not in love with her boss.

Delaying as long as she could, Jordan stretched out her final tasks, not wanting to appear eager to see Cade, merely because she hadn't seen him in days. She had spoken briefly to him on the phone—it wasn't enough.

Finally, at close to five, she shut off the computer, turned on the answering machine and headed for the house. She'd check on Caleb, change for dinner, and try to contain her impatience until she saw Cade again.

It wasn't necessary. As soon as she approached Caleb's room, she could hear the deep rumble of Cade's voice.

"So how come you don't have a little girl anymore?" Caleb asked.

Jordan quickened her step. She hoped Cade wouldn't blast her son with some scathing answer. Caleb was just a little boy.

She couldn't hear the words, but the tone was quiet. Pausing at the doorway, she surveyed the scene before her. Amelia was sitting in the rocker next to Caleb's bed. Cade was perched on the edge, with what looked like an entire army of action heroes spread out on the bed around Caleb.

"...accident."

"Wasn't she wearing her seat belt?" Caleb asked, his one visible eye wide as he stared at Cade.

"Yes, both she and her mother were wearing their seat belts. But the crash was too severe. It wasn't enough to save them."

Amelia had tears in her eyes. Jordan swallowed, wondering how they had arrived at this conversation. She ached for the sorrow in Cade's voice, for the tears Amelia shed, and for the tragic loss of a young life.

"Maybe I could be your new little boy. Then you wouldn't be so lonely," Caleb said.

"Caleb."

Jordan stepped inside. Time to nip that kind of thinking in the bud.

"Hi Mommy. Did you know Cade had a little girl, but she died?"

"I knew. It's sad, isn't it?"

Cade rose and turned.

She nodded in greeting. "I didn't know to expect you back today."

"Change of plans. I have to go to LA. I want you to come with me."

He gave no hint of the passion they'd shared, of the heat

and excitement of his kiss. He was her boss, merely reacting to business needs.

"Go with you? I can't. I have Caleb."

"Whom Amelia and Rosita dote on and care for as if he were their own. No harm will come to the boy."

"I've never really been away from Caleb."

She looked at her son, her heart swelling in love. The bandages were due to be removed next week. The prognosis was outstanding. She knew Amelia and Rosita loved watching him. Even so, it was a lot to ask of a mother who had never spent the night away from him before his hospital stay.

"A couple of days at most. He'll be fine."

"Now dear, don't worry about Caleb. We'll watch him like he was our own," Amelia said, rising and brushing down the flowing skirt of her soft peach dress. Her white hair was neat even after a day of watching a mischievous four-year-old. She smiled at Caleb.

"We'll have fun while your mom is away, won't we?"

"Where are you going?"

A hint of panic touched her son's voice.

"On a business trip to Los Angeles," Cade said, his gaze never leaving Jordan. "I'll tell you what, Caleb. If you're good, I'll have Joe bring in one dog so you can see him while we're gone?"

"Every day?"

Jordan hid a smile and felt a small pang. Her son was not above negotiating. She wasn't sure how to feel knowing a dog would make up for her being gone.

"Every day."

"Okay. Bring me back a present," he loftily commanded his mother.

"We'll see. Nothing's been decided," she said.

"I know it's short notice. Penny always keeps a suitcase packed for just such sudden trips. Can you be ready by morning?" Cade asked.

Jordan shook her head.

"I don't have any clothes that would be appropriate. All I brought were jeans and shorts—and only enough for a few days. I didn't know at the time I'd be here so long."

It seemed another lifetime that she'd arrived and been so disappointed not to find Caleb's father. Now she had a difficult time even remembering what he looked like or what appeal he'd had for her five years ago.

"You can pick up some things once we get there. I booked us on the nine am. flight. We have reservations for a suite at the Innsbrook on Wilshire Boulevard. With any luck, we'll finish in two days and home that night."

Jordan had a hard time concentrating on anything after the word suite. It conjured up memories of the last suite they shared—with Amelia. Only this time, it would be only the two of them. When she realized Cade and Amelia were both looking at her oddly, she nodded.

"Fine. I'll be ready first thing tomorrow."

Afraid to give away her thoughts, she turned to head for her room with a murmured "see you in a bit" for Caleb.

Cade stopped her before she reached the door.

"Jordan?"

She stopped, turned. He came closer until she breathed in

the scent of his aftershave mingled with the masculine scent that was Cade's own. Heat from his body enveloped her and she tried desperately to remember he was her boss, nothing more.

"You are not worried about traveling with me, are you?" he asked.

"Should I be?"

Her heart was pounding. She hoped he couldn't tell. Feeling much like a schoolgirl with a first crush, she tried to compose her thoughts and her features to hide any sign. How embarrassing for both of them if Cade ever suspected how she felt about him.

"No. I had Jasmine reserve a suite for convenience. You'll have your privacy and I'll have mine. But if I need work done late at night, then it would be better for both of us to be readily available."

"I understand."

She waited a moment, but he said nothing further.

"I'll see you at dinner," she said and escaped into the bedroom.

Leaning against the door, she rested her head on the wooden panels. He'd have his room, and she'd have hers, but they'd still be close. As close as they were in this house, but with no one else around who knew them.

Maybe she should make up an excuse and stay here.

But the thought of traveling with Cade, of seeing him in action, was too tantalizing. It wouldn't be long now before Penny would be back. Then Jordan's time in Texas would be up and she and Caleb would have to head back to Florida.

Surely she could handle a few days in Los Angeles.

Cade stared at the closed door, feeling like an idiot. He didn't have to explain why he'd booked a suite. Once there, she'd have seen the obvious advantages of working together. Not that he and Penny shared a suite when they traveled. But they had worked together for many years, so fell into a pattern.

Jordan was new to office work. She might have a question or something.

Yeah, right, he scoffed as he headed back downstairs and out to the office.

Truth be told, he didn't really need Jordan to accompany him. He could have made do with the clerical staff in the LA office. But he wanted her to go. Wanted to, what, show her off?

He stopped inside the office, staring at her desk, struck by the idea. Show her off? To whom? People who worked for him? Friends?

And to what purpose? Penny would be back soon, and Jordan's reason for being in Texas would vanish. How soon would she pack and leave?

Frowning at the mere idea, Cade continued into his office and reached for the messages piled up at his desk.

Jordan had never flown before, so she had nothing to compare with their flight to the coast. But the wide, comfortable seats were a delight. Of course, Cade only traveled first-class.

She felt woefully under dressed in her faded jeans and yellow top. Most of the passengers in first class were obviously businessmen and women wearing dress-for-success suits and carrying laptops and leather briefcases.

She should have refused to travel, she thought as she slid down in her seat, glad she was by the window. Gazing out the small opening, she tried to imagine herself somewhere else. She hoped no one was looking at her, wondering what she was doing on board.

"You're not feeling sick, are you?" Cade asked.

She shook her head, her gaze fixed on the men loading baggage into the plane.

"Did you bring something to read?" he asked.

She shook her head.

"What did you expect to do on the flight?"

She looked at Cade.

"I don't know. What do you usually do?"

"Work."

"You work all the time."

"It gets me through the day," he said.

"So tell me what's so important about the Los Angeles situation you have to go there in person," she invited.

Cade hesitated only a moment, then, as if assured of her interest, explained the personnel and production crisis that he wanted to change. Soon he began explaining the entire operation to her.

Jordan was fascinated. She'd picked up bits and pieces as she'd worked for him, but to have him explain the connections and the relationship of the people she'd spoken with, it became clear he ran a complex business consortium, and ran it well.

"And the ranch, that's such a small part of everything."

"It's been my family's home for several generations, but I never wanted to be a full-time rancher. I enjoy participating in the branding, the roundup, and directing how we're going to rotate fields, which bull to try next, but my heart isn't in it completely. Not like my father's."

"That's so sad."

"What is?"

"To think it's been in your family for so long and after you, there's no one."

He looked startled, then pensive.

"Not in the direct line, but I have cousins. My grandparents are their grandparents and great-grandparents who owned the land, too. They're family."

She nodded in agreement, afraid she'd spoken out of turn. The love he had for his home shone through when he spoke of it. It might rival his love for business, but nothing would dislodge it. How sad to have no children to leave the legacy to. No one to share in the love of the land that had been part of their family for generations.

They were more than halfway to LA when he turned the tables and asked her about her life in Florida.

Jordan wasn't sure how much he really wanted to know, so glossed over many things, telling him about working at Joe's Fish Tacos, and about Caleb's love for the ocean.

"Your friend Julie's name comes up frequently, when you talk," Cade commented at one point. "But no man's. Do you have a special male friend? Or are you still waiting for Caleb's father?"

Jordan shook her head.

"No time nor inclination for men—new or old."

"Why not? You're young and pretty. I'd think the young men in South Beach would flock around."

"I've never had a flock," she replied quietly. "And dating a single mother isn't as glamorous as dating a swinging single with no attachments in a beach town."

"Their loss."

She smiled, warmed by the comment. For several seconds, her eyes locked with his. In another time, another place, would they have found they had anything in common? Would the attraction she felt flare whenever he was around grow into something shared by both of them? Should she even mention she no longer thought of Caleb's father except to let him know he had a son? Why would Cade care?

Wishful thinking. She'd tried happy-ever-after with the man she had once known as Cade Cullen Everett. He was nothing like the real thing. She didn't know who he had been, or where he was now, but she was grateful she'd had the chance to meet Cade.

"We'll go shopping when we reach LA Rodeo Drive has some nice stores."

"Rodeo Drive."

Even she had heard of the ritzy, trendy thoroughfare renowned through the world for expensive luxuries.

"I think a more traditional department store would suit better," she said.

"Since the need for clothes is business related, the company will pick up the tab," Cade said casually.

"I can't let you buy my clothes. You've already done so

much with Caleb."

"Don't argue, Jordan. It's a business related expense, all right? You wouldn't need anything if you weren't helping me with the work here. I don't care to discuss the matter any more."

Several hours later, when they finally checked into the Innsbrook Hotel, Jordan was tired, hungry and secretly elated with the selections she'd chosen. The suit would be perfect for job interviews, if she followed through when she returned to Florida. There were three separate tops to wear with it, two in cream and one in flaming red.

And the dress Cade had insisted she needed for the dinner meeting planned was daring and darling. She'd never owned anything so glamorous, yet the salesclerk continued to call it a subdued little black dress that would go from work to date with a few accessories, which she then sold as a package complete with shoes.

"I'll order a snack for us from room service while you change," Cade said when they entered the lavish suite. "As soon as we're done, we'll head for the office—before the traffic gets any worse."

"The traffic could get worse?"

"When it's rush hour, they open the shoulders as another lane and it's still backed up for miles in every direction. Wear the suit tomorrow. We'll be having dinner with the Wilsons and the Turners. We'll probably work through dinner tonight, order something to be delivered to the office."

Jordan took her time dressing, wanting to make sure she looked the part of a competent personal assistant to Cade

Everett. When she stepped from her room into the sitting area, she felt more sophisticated than ever before.

Cade frowned when he looked at her.

"Doesn't it suit me?" she asked.

"You look remote, older. Not like at home."

"I'm your efficient, competent secretary. How will people respect that if I look like a kid wearing jeans?" she countered.

Amusement lit his eyes.

"Efficient and competent, huh?"

She flushed. "Well, I want to look the part, at least."

"You've done well, especially for someone without a secretarial background. Come have something to eat. I want to leave soon."

The rest of the day passed in a whirl. Jordan met the key players at the Los Angeles office. While there were some brief comments made about Penny's absence, she'd already talked to most of the staff on the phone, so they knew to expect her. She didn't try to do more than she knew how. The others respected her for it and were more than helpful.

Cade was in his element. She watched, fascinated, as he took control, without blatantly stepping on toes. There was no question the other men respected his business savvy and took their direction from him.

When they talked about multi-million dollar mistakes, her eyes widened. Focusing on the notebook and notes she was taking for Cade, she tried to adjust her thinking. The man was far wealthier than she'd suspected if this was merely one portion of the many companies he directed. No wonder funding Caleb's operation hadn't been a hardship for him.

She still planned to repay him, but more from her own sense of honor than any need for money on his part.

Jordan fell asleep immediately after her head hit the pillow later that night. The day had started early in Texas and ended late in California. Did he keep up such a hectic pace normally?

She gave no thought to Cade, only a room away. Grateful for the break, she slept through the night without interruption.

Cade checked his watch once again. It was after seven and he had not heard a single sound from Jordan's room. Their breakfast would arrive soon.

He walked to the window and drew open the drapes. LA was on the move, cars and buses crowding the streets, the high morning fog from the sea mere wisps of gray against a pale blue sky.

He walked to her door and listened. Nothing. Knocking softly, he waited. Had she wakened earlier and gone out for a walk?

Cade turned the knob and pushed the door open slightly, peering into Jordan's room. She was still fast asleep, on her side, her face resting on one hand like a child.

Stepping in, he watched her sleep for several seconds. She looked younger, more like the Jordan he'd come to know over the last few weeks than the woman who had worn the trappings of a corporate employee yesterday.

That had startled him. He never noticed what Penny wore. She was always suitably turned out for whatever meeting or social event they attended. Yet on Jordan, it had looked artificial.

He liked the way she normally looked, he realized. Like now, her skin flushed from sleep, her hair in disarray around her head. The soft rise and fall of her breasts as she slept drew his eyes.

Desire hit him like a powerful punch. He wanted her as he had wanted no one in a long time. Maybe ever. She was a pretty woman, but not beautiful. She seemed so innocent despite having a child and working on her own for several years. Maybe it was because of the hardships she'd survived that he admired her so much.

Or because of her cheerful attitude despite difficulties that would overwhelm another person.

He enjoyed having her in his life, he realized. Even Caleb was growing on him, despite his vow to remain apart from potentially hurtful situations.

"Jordan?" he called softly.

She didn't stir. Cade noted it for future reference—Jordan slept deeply and wasn't easy to awaken.

"Jordan?"

His voice louder, he entered her room and crossed to the bed. Hesitating only a moment, he placed his hand on her shoulder, registering instantly the warmth of her soft skin, the silky texture. Shaking her gently, he left his hand there, absorbing the feel of her against his palm.

"Jordan, it's time to get up. We have a lot to do today."

Her eyes came open slowly. For a moment, he recognized her confusion. Then she met his gaze and looked startled. Reluctantly, Cade removed his hand, wishing he could come up with a reason not to.

"How late is it?"

She sat up. Suddenly aware of the barely there nightie she wore, she pulled the sheet up to her chin.

"It's after seven. Breakfast will be here any minute and I want to leave by eight."

"I'll be ready."

Cade strode from the room without a backward glance. He dare not risk further perusal of his lovely temporary secretary. The wispy nightie surprised him, though if he thought about it he couldn't say exactly why. Probably since she normally wore jeans and cotton shirts, he had expected her nightwear to be plain and practical.

She constantly surprised him. He expected her to make a play for him, but she remained aloof, unless he counted the kisses they'd shared. There had been nothing aloof about her response.

Was she playing a deep game or was she inexperienced?

Not totally, of course. She had a son after all. But there was an innocence around her that contrasted to her tough I-can-do-it-myself act. She had done well helping him out. She was devoted to her son.

And she fit in with Amelia. Even his own cousins had difficulty dealing with their aunt sometimes. But Jordan and Caleb loved being in her company.

Cade crossed to the window and gazed out over the LA landscape, mostly high-rises and freeways. He'd be glad to get back home once the situation here was wrapped up. Would Jordan?

For a moment, he toyed with the idea of offering Jordan

a job that would keep her in Tumbleweed. She and Caleb had friends in Florida, but no relatives. They could easily relocate to Texas. Caleb would grow up with horses and dogs, which all boys should be able to do.

She was touchy, however. He couldn't just make up something to hold her. It would have to be a legitimate job that didn't question her independence or smack of charity.

Room service delivered their breakfast just as Jordan emerged from her bedroom. They ate quickly and headed for the offices.

"Did you get all the notes from yesterday's meeting typed?" Cade asked as their cab moved sluggishly through the rush-hour traffic.

"I did them on one of the computers and they were to be printed by Jason's secretary first thing, so you'll have them once we arrive."

"Any problems?"

"None."

He glanced at her, noting how the suit skirt had ridden up a bit, showing more of her tanned legs than he suspected she knew. Cade grew uncomfortable, realizing that he wanted to reach out and run his fingertips along that smooth skin, feel the satiny softness, revel in the sweet texture he was sure to find.

Taking a deep breath, he looked out of the window on his side of the taxi, deliberately turning his thoughts to work and the muddle the LA office seemed to be in. But Jordan's scent tantalized, and her leaning forward from time to time to better see something had him constantly aware of her.

Maybe bringing her had been a mistake, but he'd wanted her with him. Not analyzing that closely, Cade was relieved to see the office building come into view. Work was always the answer.

Chapter Eight

By six o'clock Jordan wanted to go back to the hotel, take a hot bath, and go to sleep for twelve hours. Cade was incredible. He knew more than she could ever remember, from employees' names and family situations, to the sales figures for the last several years, to the labor disputes and settlements that had been part of the company's history going back to its inception. She tried to keep up, but was lost more than half the time.

And what really annoyed her was Cade looked as fresh and raring to go this late in the day as he had that morning. He had almost as much energy as Caleb.

She slipped away from the round of farewells and placed a quick call to the ranch. It was two hours later there, and she wanted to catch Caleb before he went to bed. Chatting briefly with Amelia, she then spoke to her son. Reassured he was happy and well looked after, she reluctantly severed the connection sometime later. She missed him so much, but he was doing fine.

"Any problems?"

Cade joined her at the reception station. Closed for the day, Jordan had used that area for her phone call.

"None. Caleb's been up and around. Amelia said they were keeping him from bending over, or doing too much, but he's glad to be out of bed. Are we ready to leave?"

"I told Jim to let the Wilsons know we'll meet them all at seven thirty at Zorro's Mark. Will that give you enough time to change?"

She nodded, the dream of the hot bath fading. They'd dash back to the hotel. She'd change from the suit to that darling black dress, and then it'd be back to business.

"Don't you ever get tired?" she grumbled as she picked up her purse and the file folder of notes and reports she was keeping for Cade.

"Rarely. Are you tired?"

She straightened up and headed for the elevators.

"Not a bit," she fibbed. "But I don't keep up this pace all the time. I think I'd be exhausted if I did."

"I rest when I'm at the ranch."

She smiled at that. Some rest, riding the range, checking on the fencing, mustering cattle, not to mention fielding all the calls and emails that routinely arrived. Still making decisions that impacted every aspect of his myriad business interests.

"Something funny?"

Jordan shook her head.

"I was just wondering what you call relaxing. What would you do at the beach, organize volleyball tournaments and swim meets?"

"I don't go to the beach often."

"Too restful, huh?"

"Too far."

"Don't you take some time off from time to time? Surely you took vacations with your family."

"When my wife and daughter were alive, we went camping, and to theme parks. We even flew to the Calgary Stampede one year."

"But not the beach. Come visit us sometime. We'll see how long you can relax on the hot sand."

Jordan almost held her breath after the words were out. Would he suspect how much she wanted to keep in touch? How much she yearned for a relationship that would go beyond boss-secretary and maybe even develop into something lasting?

But Cade didn't seem unduly suspicious about her comment, merely saying maybe. Which was a non-answer if she ever heard one.

When they arrived at the trendy restaurant later that evening, Jordan felt she was entering a dreamworld. The decor was lovely, expensive, with plenty of space around each table, not crowded together like at Joe's Fish Tacos to accommodate as many customers at one time as possible.

There was even a dance floor at one end and a soft combo playing in the background.

When one of the men began to speak of work, Cade raised an eyebrow.

"Since we have our partners with us, who probably would be bored to tears with business discussions, let's keep the topics of general interest."

Jordan was surprised at his courtesy. She herself had thought it a business meeting. She enjoyed the evening, even more so when she and the others discussed Florida beaches versus Southern California ones. That led to friendly banter about all the amenities in the two states.

Only when the talk veered to children did Jordan glance at Cade, wondering if she should deflect the conversation. She knew how much he ached for his own daughter. Would a discussion of soccer and dolls be too distressing?

He surprised her by relating an episode with Caleb and the dogs at the ranch which had everyone chuckling. He didn't look devastated, didn't look as if he was going to leave the table if the conversation didn't change. She watched warily and was startled when he gave her a wink. Blushing, she looked away. Cade could fully handle his own emotions, she admitted. If he didn't like the topic, he'd change it.

When the meal was finished, Cade ordered after dinner brandy and coffee for everyone.

"Since the music is so appealing, I think it's time for some dancing."

"Oh, man, do you know how much I hate to dance?" Bart Wilson groaned.

His wife laughed in delight. "Hey, I hear an order from the big boss man. Up and at 'em, Bart."

The man made a show of reluctance, but his grin let everyone there know he was teasing her.

When Jim and his wife rose, Cade turned to Jordan. "Shall we?"

She could no more refuse him than she could refuse a request from Caleb. To be held in his arms while they danced would be the best part of the evening. Feeling daring, she nodded. She'd enjoy it as long as she didn't give herself away. She couldn't let Cade know how much she enjoyed being with him.

His hand on her back was warm, sending tendrils of awareness shivering through her. Pulling her close, he held her like a precious, fragile object, one to be cherished. For a long moment, Jordan closed her eyes, savoring every aspect of being held in Cade's arms.

The music was slow and dreamy. They moved in time with the rhythm, brushing thighs, pressing chest to breast, caught up in a world of two. Jordan felt as if she were on full alert, catching every nuance of the evening, from Cade's heady scent to the warmth of his hand against her back.

This is what life should be, she thought, two people who loved each other taking delight in being together. The quiet times alone were the best. She spared a moment of thought for Marissa and Vicki. She'd never know them, but she could feel them in Cade. Could he ever forget them and move on? Or not forget, but still make a new life—different, but just as good?

"I'm ready to head for the hotel," he whispered in her ear. "How about you?"

"If you want."

Disappointment crashed down. He'd only done a duty dance. Now that it ended, he wanted to leave. She'd been fooling herself for too long. Time for a reality check.

Cade urged the others to stay. With a few last-minute instructions to his colleagues, they said goodbye. In the morning, Cade and Jordan would return to Texas.

To Jordan's surprise, when they reached the hotel, Cade stopped her as she headed for the elevator.

"They have a dance floor in the lower level bar of the hotel. Care to have a nightcap and dance a little longer?"

"I thought you were tired."

Jordan couldn't hide her surprise. Or the sudden surge of happiness that swept through her.

"Actually, I wanted to ditch the others and thought that excuse was a diplomatic way to handle it—and hopefully not give rise to gossip."

"Why would there be gossip?"

"Anyone looking at us dancing together would immediately suspect we are something more than boss and PA."

"They would?" Her heart kicked into high speed. "Why?"

"Because there is something more, and only a blind man would miss it. Dance?"

"Yes, please."

The dance floor in the hotel bar was almost empty. Only two other couples took advantage of the hotel's ensemble. When Cade swept her into his arms, Jordan knew she never wanted the night to end. Caleb and her job and her life in Florida seemed to fade into the background. The evening had taken a surreal aspect, as if she were new and free and floating on gossamer wings. Cade filled her senses, setting her aflame with what could be, what might be.

She loved Cade Everett. It differed from anything she'd ever experienced. And much stronger and more mature than the feelings she once thought she had for Caleb's father.

She loved dancing with Cade. Every brush of his body put hers on high alert. Every caress with his fingertips on the bare skin of her back had erotic images dancing in her mind and cranked up the awareness another notch.

She loved talking with him, hearing his views on issues, feeling the soft laughter when something stuck him funny—which was rare. He more often had a lurking sadness in his eyes. She cherished the amusement when she saw it, happy she could put it there.

She loved being with him, to savor the moments, to explore the scant time they had together before it all ended.

She felt like Cinderella at the ball, only there would be no magic glass slipper, no happily ever after ending. Her prince wasn't searching for a wife, but mourning one.

And she didn't have a fairy tale godmother. One look at her situation would convince anyone of that.

But like Cinderella must have done at the ball, Jordan cherished every second. At least she'd have the memories to last all her days.

It was late when they finally moved to the elevators. Jordan felt wrapped in a time warp, almost afraid to say anything lest the mood shatter and she had to face reality. A few more moments until she was in bed and she could relive each moment of the evening, imprinting it on her mind to remember forever.

"I had such a wonderful time," she said dreamily as the elevator doors closed. "I think I love LA."

He pulled her against him in the empty elevator, his arm on her shoulder, his fingers rubbing light circles on her shoulder.

"Better than Tumbleweed?" he asked.

"Mmmm, maybe not. I like the ranch, Amelia, Rosita." She stopped before she said too much.

When they reached the suite, Cade opened the door. The lights had been turned off, only the sparkling lights beyond the window illuminated the room.

"How pretty," Jordan exclaimed at the sweep of lights as far as the eye could see.

"As pretty as you are," Cade said, closing the door behind them and turning her in his arms.

When his mouth covered hers, Jordan gave herself up to his kiss. She yearned for him, craved his touch, longed for more. She'd been lonely, but he filled the void and brought happiness. She'd been alone, but with him felt as if two parts of a whole had come together.

Winding her arms around his neck, she opened her mouth when his tongue caressed her lips and danced with his when he swept in. She was glad for his strong arms as her bones seemed to soften and melt. If he wasn't holding her, she'd probably collapse on shaky knees.

Time spun away. There was only this moment, only the surging sensations that built and built. Jordan reveled in them, awed by the power of passion as it grew, amazed at the desire that rose with each second. Oh, if only it could last a lifetime.

"I want you, Jordan," he murmured, kissing her cheek, trailing nibbling kisses along her jaw, tilting back her head to lick and kiss down her neck to that rapid pulse point at the base of her throat.

"Stay with me tonight."

Her heart leapt at his words. He wanted her as much as she wanted him. Had he gotten over his wife? Was he ready to move on—with her?

"I want you, too, Cade," she said, burning with desire and longing. She tightened her own hold, drawing him closer.

He bent and lifted her into his arms, cradling her against his chest.

"I don't believe it," she murmured, reaching up to kiss him along the jaw. "This only happens in movies."

He captured her lips with his as he walked easily into his bedroom. The lights from outside allowed him to see the shape and location of the bed. Gently settling her on the mattress, he slipped off her shoes, kneeling on the floor in front of her.

Jordan wished she could see him, see what his eyes said, see his expression. Lacking sight, she relied on touch. His fingertips trailed up her leg, slipping beneath the skirt of the dress, trailing fire and ice in their wake. His voice was raspy when he spoke.

"No regrets, Jordan."

It felt like a dash of cold water.

This wasn't her dream come true. It was one night out of time. A special night for just the two of them. But it wasn't a vow for the future, nor a promise she could hold on to. He'd never even hinted before that he was interested in her as a woman.

"None," she replied, leaning over to frame his face in her palms, and kissed him again.

"But I decline."

With determination, she rose and circled around him, making her way quickly to her bedroom and firmly closing the door behind her. She couldn't believe she hadn't taken him up on his suggestion. She'd love to spend the night with him, and the afternoon and early morning. But not like this.

She had experience with someone who said he loved her and left. Cade was clear there was no love involved. There was no future.

Jordan got ready for bed, wishing she had some way to contact Penny to see when the woman was returning. The sooner Caleb and she could return to Florida, the better.

Daylight poured into the bedroom when Cade opened his eyes. He stacked his hands behind his head and gazed at the ceiling. Last night, he had made a mess of things. He hoped Jordan would speak to him today.

His wife had been dead for two years. The first time he'd taken a woman out after Marissa's death, he'd been consumed with guilt. The few dates he'd tried had been disasters. He had compared everyone to Marissa.

He'd insisted Jordan accompany him to Los Angeles as an experiment. He found her appealing and fascinating. But he wasn't sure he was ready to move on from his wife.

Had last night been another test? Had he wanted to see how he felt sleeping with another woman? Or had he really wanted to become intimate with Jordan for herself?

Surprised, he realized he wanted her. He'd love to make love to her in the sunshine that was spilling into the room. He'd look into her eyes and see all the emotions she felt as they explored this new step.

And then what?

He shied away from thinking about the future.

No regrets, Cade had said last night. But as Jordan stood by the window in her room, later, she had a boatload of regrets. She tried to tell herself she hadn't expected a declaration of undying devotion. That she hadn't expected him to fall madly in love with her.

But she had lied to herself.

She wanted his love. She ached with her own love for him. Wished she was free to tell him, to touch him when she wished, to close the door when just the two of them were in a room and kiss him silly.

But that was the fantasy. He never gave a hint he wanted anything beyond a one-night stand.

And that was not who Jordan was.

Last night had been a magical evening out of time. But reality resumed. They had a flight to Dallas to catch, and would be back at the ranch before dinner.

She'd called a few moments ago and spoken with Caleb. He was her primary concern. Love for her son filled her heart. She'd cherish her memories of Los Angeles, but move on as she had when she'd discovered Caleb's father's perfidy.

How soon before Penny returned? Before she'd leave and never see Cade Everett again? How would she bear walking away without a backward look?

But it beat being around him and knowing he was not for her.

Why couldn't he love her as she loved him?

Yet how could she ever compete with a dead woman? The perfection of that relationship couldn't compare with her and the baggage of her past.

Ready at the designated time, Jordan wore her new suit, as if donning armor to aid in her defenses. She wouldn't hint at the turmoil that roiled inside her. She was his temporary secretary and would act the role. Determined to carry it off, she stepped into the sitting room.

Cade stood near the window, studying the view. The famous Los Angeles smog had returned, the hazy air shimmering in the early morning heat. He turned when she entered, and Jordan was glad she'd dressed in her new role when she saw the remote expression on his face.

"Ready?" he asked.

At her nod, he lifted the phone and called for a bellman and requested a cab.

"I called Caleb," she said as they waited awkwardly. Fiddling with the strap on her handbag, she glanced out the window, finding that easier than facing him.

"He's doing well. Says nothing hurts anymore, and he wants to go riding."

"Once the doctor gives the go ahead, we'll see about putting him up on a gentle mount."

She nodded, wondering if they'd still be at the ranch when the bandages came off. She mustn't forget their stay there was so temporary.

"Jordan—"

A knock at the door interrupted Cade's statement. The bellman had arrived to take their luggage.

Any private conversation was impossible from then on. In no time, they were dropped off at the curb at Los Angeles International Airport. Once they were through the security checks, Cade suggested they get something to eat, since their flight departure was still more than an hour away.

Jordan had no appetite, but since they hadn't eaten since dinner last night, she knew she had to give the appearance at least.

The trip home seemed endless. Jordan took two magazines on the plane with her and read them from cover to cover. Cade seemed no more eager to talk about last night than she did, engulfing himself in work, using the in-flight phone to touch base with the Dallas office and reaffirm some decisions made in Los Angeles.

Once in his car, she feigned sleep to avoid any conversation. She knew it was cowardice, but she couldn't help it. She needed to gain some distance before she could deal with the situation.

Of course, she'd feel totally different if he gave the slightest sign that she was someone special to him. But from his demeanor today, she deduced he had regrets at suggestion the liaison. His remote attitude drove her crazy, and she refused to open the discussion for fear of what she might say or hear.

Once home, she almost ran to Caleb's bedroom. Hugging him when she dashed into the room, she felt her world stabilize. Here was her reality. Not some fairy tale dream come true with Cade, but her precious son who needed her and whom she loved so much.

"I missed you, Mommy," Caleb said.

"I missed you, too, sweetheart."

She shrugged out of her suit jacket and tossed it over the end of the bed, perching beside Caleb.

"Tell me all you did."

"Hi, Cade," Caleb said.

Jordan looked at the man leaning casually against the doorjamb. Her heart caught as it normally did every time she saw him. She hadn't expected him to follow her.

"Hi Caleb. How are you doing?"

"I'm almost all better. Aunt Amelia said if I had any more energy, they'd have to bottle it to sell." He almost bounced on the bed. "Rosita has games we played. Candyland is my favorite—only you don't get any real candy. And there's Chutes and Ladders. Her grandchildren play them and so I got to, too. And Aunt Amelia taught me how to play Go Fish. Can we play cards, Mommy? I'm really good. Aunt Amelia said I'm a natural."

Jordan nodded and laughed at his exuberance, all the while conscious of Cade's brooding presence in the doorway. She flicked a glance at him from time to time, wondering what he was thinking. She hadn't expected him to stay through Caleb's recitation. And his expression was anything but comfortable. But he didn't leave.

"Sounds like so much fun. We'll have to get cards to take home with us," she said, wondering where she could also find the games. Maybe at a store in town. Otherwise, she'd have to wait until they returned to South Beach.

"I'm sure we have a few decks lying around. Caleb can

have a couple," Cade said.

Jordan looked at him, struck by how lonely he looked. Standing in the doorway as if looking in on something, he couldn't quite join.

She longed to ask him to come sit on the bed, to tell Caleb about their trip, but dare she? If she did, what would he think? That she was trying to make more of their relationship than there was? Or did he just want to be included?

"Come in and tell Caleb about card games you played as a child," she said, daring to try.

For a moment she thought he'd join them. Then he straightened.

"I have work to do," he said, turning to leave.

Jordan's heart sank. She had hoped.

"Mommy, I got to play with a dog. Mr. Murray brought him in. Rosita didn't like it, but Aunt Amelia said it was all right. He didn't have a tail, but he wiggled all the time, and licked me."

"I wish I had been here. Did you like the dog?"

She tried to focus on Caleb's animated descriptions of the cattle dog who had visited, but part of her wondered about Cade. Had he gone to change? Would he head for the office? Or just close himself away in the study?

Already the trip to Los Angeles was fading.

Amelia waited for Jordan to join her in the dining room before beginning dinner. Jordan still wore the skirt and blouse from the flight and was pleased Amelia liked it.

"Not as feminine and flowery as the dresses you like," Jordan said, slipping into her place at the table.

"Ah, I do like my frilly dresses," Amelia said with a satisfied smile. "But they're not for everyone. That outfit suits you and makes you look older, more mature. How did you fare in Los Angeles? It's been an age since I was there. If we had all gone, we could have taken Caleb to an amusement park while Cade worked."

"I went to help Cade," Jordan reminded her gently.

When Rosita entered carrying a platter of roast beef surrounded by new potatoes, Jordan smiled at her.

"I hear I have you to thank for hours of fun Caleb had playing board games."

"He's a delightful child. If he's here when my grandchildren come to visit, they will play well together."

"Why wouldn't he be?" Amelia asked. "And as soon as the bandages come off and they make sure his eye set, he'll be rearing to go. Jack said he could help groom one of the gentler horses, if that is okay with you, Jordan. I don't see why not. Vicki had her own pony by this age, though she didn't take care of it all by herself. That would be too much for a child, only four. But she could ride with a lead and loved to visit and talk with that pony. And feed it carrots. Remember, Rosita?"

"Indeed, I do, Señorita. I will bring the rolls."

Cade's place had been set, but he hadn't arrived.

"Caleb said you taught him how to play Go Fish," Jordan said as they ate.

"Vicki loved to play card games on a rainy day. She and Marissa or she and Cade or all three of them. Especially in the wintertime when Cade didn't work outside, or have to go into Dallas. They'd fix popcorn and spend the afternoon in front of the fire."

The older woman grew pensive.

"I shall always miss them. They went far before their time."

Jordan nodded, wondering if that was what Cade had seen at Caleb's bedroom door—an echo of the times he and his wife played cards with their daughter. No wonder he hadn't wanted to come in and join them.

It was obvious he didn't plan to join them for dinner, either. Jordan tried to ignore the empty place, tried to focus on what Amelia was saying, but in her mind she felt sadness for the man. If there was only something she could do to ease the pain of his loss.

The next morning, Jordan dressed in her usual jeans and pullover top. She had work to do. She refused to dwell on fantasies that remained out of reach.

When she entered the office, she stopped in surprise. An immaculately groomed woman sat behind her desk. She looked up when Jordan entered.

"You must be Jordan Carhart."

"And you're Penny."

Jordan's heart dropped. There had been no warning. Penny had returned as unexpectedly as she'd left.

"Cade rode out early this morning. I arrived just before he left," Penny said.

She glanced around the desk.

"You have done adequately in my absence. Of course, he told me you weren't trained in secretarial work, which explains a lot."

Jordan flushed with embarrassment. She'd done her best. Cade had no complaints once she mastered the computer and phone. But she knew she'd never achieve all his paragons of a personal assistant had. And now Penny had returned.

"I hope things are all right here. And that your mother has recovered," Jordan said.

"The filing's up to date and the correspondence logged. I'll find my way around. My mother's recovering. Her sister is going to stay with her. So I've returned."

It was a dismissal, loud and clear.

"I'll be at the house. Let me know if you can't find anything," Jordan said, turning around abruptly and retracing her steps head held high.

There was no reason to remain on the ranch or in Texas beyond tomorrow when Caleb had the bandages removed. Their doctor in Florida could well take care of him over the next few months. Thanks to Cade's generosity, Jordan still had most of her surgery funds, which should cover medical follow-up expenses.

Of course, there was still the matter of owing him for the operation, but she'd deal with that once she was back home and sure about a job. Maybe she could work out a repayment plan. It'd only take two or three lifetimes at her wages. Still, something might turn up.

After Penny's comments, however, she might reevaluate her desire for office work. Maybe she wasn't cut out for that after all.

She entered the house and went up to her room. The lilac room, not the rose room, which might have made her look flushed. She smiled sadly, remembering Amelia's convoluted conversation that first day. She'd miss her so much.

Drawing her suitcase from the back of the closet, she began to pack. She'd take care of Caleb's clothes next and they could drive to Dallas in the morning, have the surgeon check him and then head for Florida. With any luck, her old car wouldn't break down on the return trip and they'd be home within a few days.

She'd have to call Joe and see if she still had a job. Once home, she planned to look into community college courses in business. She enjoyed working in an office. If she could find the time, she'd like to learn more.

Gently folding her business suit, she brushed her fingers over the soft material. It'd be perfect for interviews once she had some skills. Every time she wore it, she'd remember Cade and their whirlwind trip to Los Angeles.

Would Cade give her a reference?

"What are you doing?"

Cade stood in the doorway, holding a Stetson in one hand. His jeans were dusty, his boots muddy. Jordan could smell horses and cattle from where she stood. And her heart flipped over.

"Packing. Penny's back."

"I saw her before I went out to check on the bore that's giving us trouble. She said you had come to the office, but she hadn't needed help."

He looked at the opened suitcase. "Leaving?"

"I thought it best. You don't need me anymore now that Penny's here. I'll take Caleb into Dallas tomorrow for the follow-up visit to the surgeon, then head for home."

He stared at her for a long moment.

Jordan wanted to fidget under his gaze, but held onto her composure. Unable to meet his eyes, however, she resumed folding and packing.

"Don't go."

Cade said in such a low voice she thought she had imagined it.

"What?"

She looked up. He was studying the carpet.

"Don't go. Stay here. We'll find something for you to do."

She hadn't imagined it.

"Like what? I'm no cowboy. And we both know I was a makeshift secretary. I'd need more training if I wanted to do that full time. You don't need more than Penny here. Each office has a full staff. There'd be nothing for me to do."

"We'll find something."

"I can't stay. We've imposed enough."

And she didn't want to feel like a charity case. She hoped she'd pulled her weight at the office. But there was nothing left for her to do.

"You haven't imposed. Caleb likes it here. Amelia enjoys having him around. He's almost old enough to have a pony."

"Which I can't afford."

Why was he making it so hard?

"But I can," Cade said.

She shook her head at his stubbornness and arrogance. Just because he could, didn't make it right for her to accept.

"We are already in your debt for the operation."

"You helped me out when I needed it. Consider us even."

Jordan didn't consider them anywhere close to even, but she would not argue with him. Once home, she'd figure out how much she could pay each week and send the money.

"You didn't get to go to college. Stay and take some classes. See if you still want to be an architect. Caleb can start school in Tumbleweed in the fall. Amelia and Rosita could watch him afternoons."

"Cade, I can't stay. I don't have a job, no income. My savings won't last for long, and I can't let you foot the bill for my schooling."

Caleb's operation was one thing. She'd do anything for her son, even swallow her pride. But Cade was talking about something totally different now.

"You could stay and go to college if you married me."

Chapter Nine

Now she knew she was hallucinating. She stared at him, hope blossoming. *Marriage? To Cade?*

She cleared her throat. "Marriage?"

He met her eyes and nodded.

"Marry me and stay here in Tumbleweed. Caleb loves the ranch. You like it here, you said so."

A thousand questions flooded Jordan's mind. But the happiness that exploded drove every single one away. Cade wanted her to stay—enough to marry her.

She held his gaze as she walked toward him.

"Are you sure?"

Once, long ago, she'd thought a man would want to marry her. Instead, he'd vanished from her life completely. Now she was grateful. The love she felt for Cade was far stronger than any she'd imagined for Caleb's father.

But marriage—it had been the last thing she'd expected.

He reached for her when she came near, pulling her into his embrace.

"I'm dusty and sweaty from riding," he said, looking down into her eyes.

"I don't mind a bit," she said, reaching up to kiss him.

Would she always be breathless around him, always become instantly inflamed by his kisses? She hoped so.

Winding her arms around his neck, she kissed him, pouring as much of her love into the embrace as she could. She loved him and he loved her. They were going to spend their lives together.

Wait until she told Caleb. And Amelia. And Julie.

"I love you, Cade," she whispered against his mouth.

He pulled back a bit.

"Then it's settled. We'll get married and you'll stay here. Let me take a quick shower and then we'll tell the others," he said, brushing his thumb across Jordan's damp lips. "Caleb will be delighted."

Jordan smiled, her arms still looped around his neck. He was hers. She could touch him whenever she wanted. See him whenever she wanted. She wished she could run up to the rooftop and shout the news to the world. Take an ad out in every daily paper in the country, plaster billboards with the news.

"I'm sure he'll be thrilled. But he'll pester you to death now to let him be a cowboy," she said, pleased he included Caleb in the arrangement.

She had to imagine the pain that flickered in his eyes. This was a joyful occasion.

He nodded, gently pulling her arms down. "I'll meet you for lunch and we'll tell Amelia and Caleb together."

Jordan watched him walk down the hall to his own room, wishing she dare follow him. She'd love to be there when he came out of the shower. Talk while he dressed.

She turned back to her bed and quickly unpacked. The next move would be to Cade's room, and she wouldn't need the suitcase for that.

Of course, there were her things in Florida. Maybe he'd like to take their honeymoon there and pack up her apartment. It didn't sound that romantic, but it'd be practical.

She brushed her hair, her thoughts spinning. How soon could they marry? Would he stay at the ranch more, or move them to his penthouse in Dallas? Staring at the bright color in her face, she just grinned, letting the delight blossom in her heart. *Cade loved her.*

Or did he?

She paused, brush suspended midair, suddenly realizing he'd never said the words.

But surely a man didn't ask a woman to marry him if he didn't love her. Guys weren't as mushy as women. Hadn't she always heard that? Of course, he loved her.

She stared at herself in the mirror, doubts crowded in. He had to love her. She loved him so much she couldn't stand it if he didn't love her back.

But he hadn't said the words.

And she had—loud and clear.

Was he shy? She almost laughed, except fear gripped her. She couldn't picture Cade shy about anything. So why hadn't he said the word back?

Because he didn't love her.

He was still in love with his first wife. Jordan was just— what? A convenience? Or was he offering her a place to live for some other reason?

Cade made the announcement at lunch as soon as they sat, with Rosita present. Jordan hadn't talked to him and couldn't now with everyone bubbling over with the news. But later, she'd corner him later and get some answers. In the meantime, she put on a cheerful face and tried not to let the doubts and fears gain dominance.

"Oh, my dear," Amelia rose instantly and came to give Jordan a hug. "I'm so delighted."

She moved to kiss her nephew and then Caleb.

"Are you my daddy now?" Caleb asked.

"I'll be your stepfather," Cade replied.

"And we get to live here forever and ever?" Caleb persisted.

"Yes, forever and ever."

"Can I have a pony?"

Jordan laughed.

"I knew it. We'll wait to discuss that later."

Something else to talk over when they were alone. She tried to figure out what Cade's expressions meant. He didn't seem to be the happiest she'd ever seen him.

"I wish you much happiness, Señor, Señorita," Rosita said, her face wreathed in smiles.

"My goodness, after lunch, Jordan, you and Rosita and I will have to get together to make wedding plans," Amelia said when she resumed her seat. "A garden wedding, do you think? Or since you'll probably become a member of our church, would you rather have it there? Oh dear, you didn't want to have it in Florida, did you?"

"We'll probably have a judge marry us," Cade said,

reaching for the plate of biscuits.

Three pairs of eyes swung to him in dismay.

He looked up. "No?"

"It's Jordan's wedding, I think she should decide," Amelia said primly.

"It's my wedding, too," Cade said.

"I know, dear, but a second for you. This is her first."

"And only one, I hope," she murmured, struck by the questions that wouldn't leave.

Why had he asked her? It was likely Cade didn't want to do anything to remind him of his first wedding. Had it been a garden wedding? Or a formal affair held in the church?

He never spoke about Marissa and rarely about Vicki. For a moment, the sunshine seemed dimmer. They needed to discuss this in private, and soon.

"We'll decide what we want and then make plans," Jordan said. "He just asked me, there are a thousand things to decide. Let us get used to the idea first."

"Very well, but it's already May, and a summer wedding is so lovely," Amelia said.

"Can I have a dog?" Caleb asked, bored with the discussion about weddings.

"We'll see," Cade said.

"Yea."

Cade raised an eyebrow and looked at Jordan. She shrugged.

"It's almost a sure thing if I say I'll see," she explained.

As soon as lunch was finished, Cade rose and excused himself, having to go to the office. He brushed a kiss on

Jordan's cheek.

"I need to talk to you," she said.

"We can talk after dinner, just the two of us."

"Sounds good," she said, her heart rate increased with his casual kiss. Just as if they were already old, married folks. She was the luckiest woman on the face of the earth. For a few hours she kept that thought in the forefront, refusing to dwell on the doubts.

After dinner, Jordan supervised Caleb's bath, careful not to let his head get wet, nor let him move suddenly, which could cause a problem with his healing eye. Once he was in bed, they talked for a while about the changes in their lives. He didn't mind leaving the ocean if he could have a dog and a pony and one day go on roundups.

Jordan was delighted her son took to the change, but wondered how strong the bond with Cade would become. Would he have time for Caleb? Or constantly be drawn to working long hours as he had in the weeks they'd lived at the ranch?

Once Caleb was settled for the night, Jordan went to find Cade. Time to talk. She wandered down to the study. Amelia had already returned to her cottage for the evening. Rosita was in her room, so it would be just the two of them, with no chance of interruption. Jordan's heart sped up in anticipation of what the two of them might find to do that went beyond discussion.

She paused in the doorway, studying the man she loved. His shoulders were broad, strong enough to support the weight of the world, she thought whimsically. His dark hair beckoned. She wanted to run her fingers through it, claiming him as hers.

He was studying a photograph. Curious, Jordan entered the room and crossed to the desk.

He looked up, his face shuttered.

"Hi," she said softly, her eyes on the picture. It was of a young girl. "Is that Vicki?"

He nodded and held the photo out for her inspection.

She'd been a darling child, bright and laughing in the pose. Jordan felt a clutch of sadness at the thought of this happy life being cut so short. She handed it back.

"She was beautiful," she said. "Do you have other pictures?"

He nodded, slipping the photograph into the top drawer of the desk.

"Ask Amelia. She kept them all. She can show you the entire clan. I'm sure she plans to invite them all to the wedding."

Jordan sat gingerly on the edge of the desk.

"If you want to just stand up in front of a judge, that would work for me."

She'd given up dreams of a white dress and a formal church wedding after Caleb's father vanished. The wedding wasn't what was important to her. The marriage was.

Cade held out his hand, and Jordan took it. He drew her over to him and settled her in his lap, resting his head on the softness of her hair. He meant to go through with the wedding.

Bleakly, he gazed off into space, holding one woman,

thinking of another wedding. Of the parties, the excitement, the surety they both had of love everlasting.

Jordan deserved the same excitement, the same happiness. She didn't know many people in Texas. It wouldn't be the same. But he wanted her to be happy. To have memories she could cherish in the years to come.

"What do you think of a garden wedding?" he asked. "Amelia will invite a few thousand guests and we could have an old-fashioned Texas-style barbecue for a reception."

"A few thousand? You're joking, right?"

The uncertainty in Jordan's voice touched him. And once again affirmed he had made the right decision.

"You know Amelia, she never met anyone who wasn't an instant friend. But I suspect thousands is a bit of an exaggeration. Maybe only several hundred. Once you get all the cousins and family, the entire town, and my business associates, it'll be a crowd. You'll have friends you want to invite."

"Few, and I doubt they'll be able to come to Texas anyway," she said slowly.

"Hey, for your wedding, we'll send them airline tickets."

She shook her head.

"Too expensive."

Cade wanted to tell her she never need worry about money again. After years of fending off relatives and acquaintances interested in that money, Jordan was a refreshing change. Was that the reason he wanted to shower her with anything she desired?

Or was it to make up for the lack in him? She wanted

hearts and flowers and love everlasting, and he had only a home to offer and the ability to provide for her son. He hoped it'd be enough. In the meantime, he'd get Penny to find out more about Jordan's closest friends and make the arrangements—once they decided on a wedding date.

"How soon would you like to get married?" he asked.

"Tomorrow," she replied promptly. "If you're sure."

"Why wouldn't I be?" he asked.

"I don't know."

She was afraid to ask if he loved her. What if he didn't? She wasn't sure she could face that.

"Why do you want to marry me, Cade?" she asked softly.

"Why do people normally marry—to spend time together, to share their lives."

"I love you, but you've never said that back to me. You don't say it at Amelia, either."

"I care for my aunt."

"And me?"

"And you."

"Love?"

"Let's not get into some philosophical discussion about love and other emotions," he said. "We'll be married. I will pledge my life to yours. You'll have stability, a home, and a place Caleb can grow up. I'll do my best by both of you."

Jordan felt a clutch in her heart. He was offering her more than she ever expected. Couldn't that be enough? Did he love her and just not want to say the words? Or had he closed himself off so much that the offer of a home was all he had to give?

What should she do? Could she take him on those terms?

"Amelia's right. We want to do this properly. We'll invite the town, friends, family and have the wedding in the garden. I'll get some of the men to expand the grassy area. If we get sod, we can have it ready by the time our wedding date rolls around. How about August first?"

"If you're sure," she said, nestled against his chest.

Maybe men just weren't as vocal about their feelings. He hadn't had to ask her. Things could turn out for the best.

And she wanted it so much. How could it be wrong?

"A pretty wedding dress for you, and new clothes for Caleb. Not a suit, but western attire. What do you think?"

"He'll love it. Especially if you suggest it."

"And I suggest you get a beautiful dress, white if you like," he said.

"With a four-year-old boy?"

"Off white, if you insist, but feminine and especially made for you."

"We'll see."

"Good, that means yes."

Jordan tipped back her head to look at him. She moved her hand to his cheek, pressing gently. He leaned forward and kissed her. She wanted something tangible to quell all the doubts that still lingered. She'd have to step out in faith that everything would turn out right.

The next morning, Jordan, Amelia and Rosita gathered in the kitchen early. Jordan and Amelia were taking Caleb in for a follow-up visit to the surgeon at ten. The women were planning on which shops to visit and what to look for now that the date and type of wedding had been decided.

As they drove into Dallas, Jordan wished Cade had come with them. Not that she needed him, but wished he could have shared the moment the surgeon unwrapped Caleb's eye and both eyes stared at her normally.

There was still therapy to do, corrective lenses to wear until the eyes grew used to tracking together, but Caleb was amenable to it all. His good mood lasted throughout the afternoon when Amelia directed them to shop after shop, to a caterer and to two florists, looking for the perfect items for the wedding.

Jordan wanted to check out some stores in Tumbleweed before making her final decisions, but she enjoyed the glamour of the clothes, the tastes of the proposed tidbits from the caterer. The ranch hands would handle the main barbecue, Amelia said.

Caleb fell asleep on the ride back to the ranch.

Jordan was almost as tired as Caleb when they arrived home. She didn't know how Amelia managed. The woman was decades older, but she seemed as energetic and raring to go as ever. Wistfully, she wished she could sleep as Caleb had. But there wouldn't be time before dinner for a nap.

At the evening meal, Cade suggested they go into Tumbleweed in the morning.

"Don't you have work to do?" Jordan asked.

"I want us to choose rings."

"Splendid. I wondered when you'd get around to that, nephew. Seems to me you had the ring in hand when you proposed to Marissa," Amelia said.

"I wasn't as uncertain of Marissa's answer as I was of Jordan's," Cade said easily. "We'll look at the jewelers in town. If you don't see something you like, we can go into Dallas."

"I'm sure they'll have just the right ring in Tumbleweed."

Jordan was thrilled he wanted to buy an engagement ring. He did care, just didn't say the words. It wasn't that long until the wedding. A plain gold band would have suited her. To have an engagement ring to show the world had to mean something.

"We'll have lunch in town."

"To celebrate. Actually, maybe you two should plan a dinner in Dallas. I'm sure the restaurants there are much better than the ones we have in Tumbleweed," Amelia said. "I could watch Caleb for you. We could have a pleasant sleep over at my cottage. Would you like that, Caleb?"

The little boy nodded agreeably.

"We'll rent a movie and watch it with popcorn and then he can sleep in Grandpa Eli's feather bed. That's a treat I remember from my girlhood."

Jordan smiled as Caleb asked questions about the feather bed. His eyes grew bigger as Amelia told about plucking goose down from geese that grandpa Eli had raised and stuffing them in the ticking. She told about the time the ticking split and feathers went everywhere.

Jordan looked to Cade to share her delight, only to find he seemed miles away, totally unaware of Amelia's story.

When he saw her gaze, he looked away.

"So, shall I plan on Caleb for tomorrow night?" Amelia asked, at the end of her story.

"Another time we'll take you up on it, but tomorrow, lunch will have to suffice," Cade said, rising. He left the table, his plate still half full.

After Caleb went to bed and Amelia returned home, Jordan went downstairs to the study. Cade retired there every evening after dinner. Would he continue to do so once they were married, or would the two of them share quiet evenings together?

"Am I interrupting?" she asked from the doorway.

"Not at all. Come in."

Cade pressed a few buttons on his computer keyboard and shut down the program.

"I was just checking my e-mail. Which I can as easily do in the morning. Tell me more about what the doctor said about Caleb's prognosis."

Jordan wished he'd hold out his hand and draw her into his lap again, but he merely leaned back in his chair and waited.

She sat on one of the other chairs near the desk and told him about her day, then asked about his. For a while, the conversation flowed.

When it wound down, Jordan hesitated to ask any of the myriad of questions she had. There was so much about Cade she wanted to know—everything, in fact. Of course, she had the rest of her life to find the answers, but she was impatient, wanting to know it all right now.

She rested her head on the back of the chair, content that she'd been able to talk with him so easily. Maybe the other questions would come up naturally.

"Tired?" Cade asked.

"I am a little," she admitted. "Amelia has lots more energy than I have. I think we visited half the stores in Dallas, and she would have covered the other half if we had had time."

"If you're tired, go to bed. We can talk more tomorrow."

Jordan rose and yawned. "Sorry. I am tired. See you in the morning."

When morning arrived, Jordan thought about their planned trip to Tumbleweed to get a ring. She glowed with happiness. What kind of ring would Cade want her to have? She liked simple settings. None of his tastes were ostentatious, so they'd probably easily agree on the ring.

Would he wear a wedding ring as well? She'd like that. Feeling possessive, she wanted the entire world to know he was hers.

She could spend the entire morning in bed dreaming about Cade and their lives together, but she had to get up. Caleb would awaken soon.

After a quick shower, Jordan went to see to Caleb. She wished she had something else to wear, but jeans would have to do. The suit from her Los Angeles trip was too formal for casual Tumbleweed, and she hadn't brought anything else from Florida.

As ten o'clock approached, Jordan grew nervous. This would be the first time anyone outside the immediate family knew of Cade's coming marriage. How would his neighbors and friends take it? They had all known his first wife and daughter. Would they draw comparisons?

Jordan wished she knew more about Marissa and the circumstance of Cade's marriage.

"Don't be silly," she told herself as she walked out into the sunshine.

"He asked me to marry him, not the other way around."

Entering the office, Jordan smiled at Penny. She noticed Cade's office door was closed. "Is Cade ready?"

"I believe so. He told me he'd be gone most of the day. I didn't offer my best wishes yesterday. I hope you both will be happy."

She rang the intercom and told Cade that Jordan was waiting to see him.

"We're buying rings," Jordan said, trying for a friendly note.

Penny looked up and nodded.

"So he said. Get a big one, he's good for it."

Jordan wandered to the door, waiting. She had called Julie first thing yesterday to share her news. Then called Joe to tell him she wouldn't be returning to Florida to live and formally giving notice to quit. What else did she need to deal with?

"Ready?" Cade came from his office. Jordan smiled, feeling that thrill she did every time she saw him. Today it felt even stronger knowing one day they'd be married and starting a life together.

"We'll be back late this afternoon," he told Penny.

Jordan noticed he wore jeans as well. Had he done so deliberately to put her at ease? Cade could be dictatorial sometimes, but he also could be surprisingly thoughtful. A complex man she was marrying.

Just before they reached town, Jordan asked if he'd wear a wedding ring.

"If you want me to," he replied.

She wanted to ask if he had with Marissa, but couldn't make herself say the words. It really didn't matter. This was their marriage, not his first one. Whether they did things the same or differently, it only mattered that they did what they wanted.

The jeweler looked surprised when Cade told him what he wanted. The glance at Jordan had her once again feeling inadequate. But she forgot it all when the man spread out a rainbow of rings on the black velvet drop cloth. The diamonds sparkled in the light. The few other precious stones contrasted with the shimmering brilliance of the diamonds.

Cade picked one and held it for Jordan's inspection. "Do you like this one?"

"It's nice."

"Lacks a ringing endorsement," he said, placing it back on the velvet. "Which do you prefer?"

She studied the display, reaching out for the simple solitary diamond in a plain gold setting.

"This one."

Despite Penny's words, Jordan wanted a ring she loved, not one to show off. She'd be wearing it the rest of her life.

He nodded to the jeweler. "We'd like to see matching wedding rings, as well."

They looked at the rings, discussing what they liked and didn't like, finally choosing matching bands with a braided motif.

Somehow, the morning fell flat.

Jordan didn't know why. She should feel thrilled to be

choosing rings for a lifetime. Maybe it was the jeweler's supercilious attitude, or Cade's lack of emotion. Somehow, there was no spark, no excitement.

And she couldn't even have her engagement ring today. It had to be sized to fit her smaller finger.

Still, she reminded herself as they left the shop, it was the marriage that counted, not the trappings.

Cade took her to the Cattleman's Club, one of the nicest restaurants in Tumbleweed. The restaurant was crowded with ranchers and local businessmen, but the hostess managed to find a quiet table for them. As they wound through the main dining room, several people called greetings to Cade. He returned them all, not stopping to introduce Jordan.

After they were seated, he looked at her.

"Time enough to get to know everyone without having to explain to everyone we meet today," he said. Glancing around the room, he continued, "Most of them will be invited to the wedding."

"It'll probably take me months to get everyone straight."

A familiar person approached. Jordan had no trouble getting Gloria straight. She braced herself, but the woman virtually ignored her.

"Cade, darling. I didn't know you were coming to town today."

With a dismissing glance at Jordan, she smiled warmly at him.

"Taking your little secretary out to lunch? How nice."

Cade had risen when she reached the table. Now he

smiled, but Jordan noticed there was no warmth in his gaze.

"Penny's returned. Jordan's no longer working for me."

"Oh?" Gloria looked surprised, but it was nothing to her expression when he added, "Jordan and I are celebrating our engagement. We're going to be married in August. You and your family will receive an invitation, of course."

"I didn't even know you were dating again," Gloria blurted.

Recovering quickly, she forced a smile onto her face and offered congratulations. Once she resumed her seat several tables away, Cade sat down.

Technically, Jordan thought as she perused the menu, this was probably their first date. Unless she counted the dinner and dancing at the business meal in Los Angeles. No wonder Gloria hadn't heard he was dating.

From the way people looked their way, Jordan knew Gloria was already spreading the news. But Cade seemed totally oblivious. Taking her cue from him, she ignored the other customers and concentrated on Cade.

As he had said, this was to celebrate their engagement. Putting on a bright smile, she set out to celebrate.

They returned home in the late afternoon, and Cade headed for the office.

"I have time to go over a few things with Penny," he said, glancing at his watch. "I'll see you at dinner."

Jordan looked for Caleb, but when she didn't find him in his room, she went to check with Rosita.

"He's over at the cottage with Señorita Amelia. She was

going to let him take a nap in that feather bed she has. I guess her stories last night made him want to sleep in it and she dotes on him. He's a lucky boy."

"We both are," Jordan said.

Caleb would have an extended family now, with Amelia and the rest of Cade's family. Aunts, uncles, cousins. Grandparents.

How would his family feel about this marriage? She hadn't even met his parents. It was a lot to think about.

Jordan walked the short distance to Amelia's cottage. She'd never been inside and was enchanted when invited in. It looked like a doll's house, with feminine Queen Anne furniture, lacy curtains, and colorful pillows everywhere. It suited Amelia to a T.

Pictures crowded the living room walls, some of Cade, others of family members she didn't as yet know. Knickknacks cluttered the tabletops and shelves, from delicate crystals, to fine bone china, to sturdier snuffboxes and carved wooden figures.

Amelia was delighted to see Jordan, and wanted to hear all about the rings they'd chosen. She was disappointed Jordan wasn't wearing the engagement ring yet.

Since Caleb was still napping, she fixed them both lemonade and brought cookies into the front room, as she called it.

Jordan crossed the room to help with the tray. She had been looking at the photographs.

"These are wonderful, all relatives? Some pictures look a

hundred years old."

"They are. My great-great-grandparents are in that stilted one there," Amelia said, pointing to one with two unsmiling individuals dressed in somber black.

"I have albums full of old pictures. I'm the only one in the family who wants them all. When everyone gets together, we spend hours going over the old albums and talking about our ancestors. But then they leave them with me. I have sorted most of them and put them in albums."

"You have pictures of Vicki, Cade said. Could I see?"

"Oh, yes. She was such a darling child. I don't guess any of us will ever entirely get over her untimely death."

Jordan took a sip of her lemonade while Amelia pulled a thick album from the lower shelf. She flipped it toward the end and pointed at the sweet little girl who smiled so sweetly into the camera.

Cade's daughter. Jordan felt a pang of sadness at the loss. How did he bear it? She didn't think she could ever endure Caleb's death.

Idly flipping through the photos, she came across one with Cade and a tall brunette, both smiling. She paused. He looked younger, different—so happy. That must be Marissa.

Jordan studied the photo. She and Marissa were nothing alike. At least he wasn't marrying her because she resembled his first wife. Marissa had been closer to Cade in age. Her healthy outdoor glow attested to her love of ranch work. Hadn't he known her all his life?

"I believe I hear Caleb. I'll go check," Amelia said.

She hurried down the hall. Jordan turned the pages again, not wanting to dwell on a woman long gone. Not wanting to think about comparing herself with Cade's first love.

Cade's only love? The insidious thought wouldn't be squelched.

She turned the page when she heard Amelia returning, her eyes instantly focused on the familiar face. Her heart almost stopped.

"It's Caleb's father," she said in stunned amazement.

Chapter Ten

"Oh, no, dear, that can't be," Amelia said, looking over Jordan's shoulder at the eight by ten wedding photograph filling the page.

"That's Cade's cousin Sam. Samuel Houston Everett. He just got married a year ago to the sweetest girl, Sara Anne Pembroke. They live in Austin. They haven't even started a family yet. And his hair is brown, not blond. Didn't you say Caleb's father was blond?"

"His hair's darker and he has a mustache now, but it's him. He told me he was Cade Cullen Everett."

Jordan was sure of it. The same sexy arrogance shone in the picture. The way he held his head, the eyes that were exactly like Caleb's. It was the man she'd known as Cade Cullen Everett five years ago on the sand at South Beach.

A cousin of Cade's. Of course, who better to know about Cade Cullen Everett and the ranch than a family member who had known him all his life? But why had he used Cade's name instead of his own?

"Oh dear. I don't know what Cade'll say," Amelia said.

Jordan studied the picture, expecting to feel something. But there was nothing. No hurt, no pain, no regrets. Any feelings she'd once held for this man had faded over the years.

She loved Cade totally and completely. Staring at this face, she felt as if she only knew him slightly, from another world. He had no place in her life, in Caleb's life. She was free of any spell he'd once held.

She looked up at Amelia.

"Don't tell him anything. He doesn't need to know."

"Oh, but he does, dear. Otherwise we'd invite Sam to the wedding and imagine how awkward that would be," Amelia said, definitely worried.

Grimly, Jordan nodded. Awkward didn't begin to describe it. How could she marry into the family unless Cade knew the truth? Would it wreck his relationship with his cousin?

What of their own relationship? How would he feel knowing she'd once loved his cousin?

Jordan knew Amelia had already told Cade by the way he stared at Caleb during dinner. And by the curt responses to any overtures on her part.

Even Amelia seemed subdued.

Rosita eyed them curiously as she served the meal. But nothing was said in front of Caleb.

Jordan felt as if they had already set a pattern for evenings. She'd put Caleb to bed, then wander down to Cade's study where they'd spend time together. Amelia usually left right before Caleb went to bed, so the rest of the evening belonged to her and Cade.

They could discuss the situation, decide what they'd do. Her heart beating fast, she headed for the study.

Tonight, she heard him talking as she approached the

door. It was almost closed, but hadn't latched. Did he have a visitor?

"...then let me hypothesize. You died your hair blond, took off for Florida on spring break when your mother and I thought you were studying to complete your course work with a passing grade. You used *my name* so no one would find out. What did you do, hock something to come up with the money?"

There was a silence. Jordan could almost feel the waves of frustration and anger. She pressed closer, knowing she shouldn't be eavesdropping, but unable to resist. Cade was talking to his cousin.

"Water under the bridge, huh? Did you never think there would be consequences for your actions?"

Another moment of silence. She wished she could hear the other person. Did he have regrets? Had it only been a careless fling for him? Would he want to know his son?

"Blast it, Sammy. I've bailed you out of trouble a dozen times since your father died. You drove your mother to distraction with your antics, always expecting someone else to pull your irons from the fire. I thought you'd turned around that last time. What of the promises you made to her? To me?"

Another silence. Jordan's heart pounded. She closed her eyes, wishing with all her heart that she'd never seen the picture, that she'd never said the fateful words aloud, or that Amelia hadn't returned at that very moment.

"Yeah, well old son, one of those wild oats is in my house right now. Along with his mother. Remember her? Jordan Carhart? Pretty blond with a figure that makes a man drool?"

Jordan hardly heard the compliment. Why had Cade called his cousin?

Shouldn't he have discussed things with her first? They could have decided together how to handle the situation.

Though she supposed a short-term solution wasn't possible. There were years of family events ahead of them. They needed to decide how to handle them all.

"While you were graduating from the university through the strings your mother and I pulled, Jordan was giving up hope of college and scrambling around to take care of your son. That counts for nothing. Her aunt died. So it was just Jordan and Caleb—and all the problems of being a single parent with no education to speak of."

Jordan's heart raced. She shouldn't be listening. But she couldn't tear herself away.

"I don't know what I want you to do, but I'm so mad I could spit nails. When are you going to take responsibility for your life, for your choices, and for your mistakes? I'm tired of bailing you out of scrapes."

Cade's hard voice sent shivers up Jordan's back. She hoped he never got that angry with her.

She caught her breath as the pain hit her. Was that what he was doing? Bailing her out? Providing a place for her because…because why? For Caleb? In memory of Vicki?

Not because he loved her. He hadn't once told her so.

And now, he had yet to mention to his cousin their upcoming wedding. Instead, he was demanding his cousin take responsibility—to relieve him of the need?

Was she living a lie?

No wonder she couldn't believe Cade loved her. He didn't, and she'd known it deep inside.

Jordan turned and almost stumbled. She froze, afraid Cade had heard her. He mustn't know she overheard his conversation. He must never suspect.

Quietly she made her way back upstairs, to her room. Closing the door softly behind her, she leaned against it, feeling old and tired and so dispirited she couldn't even begin to imagine her future.

Maybe there'd been a reason the ring hadn't been ready today. It was never to be hers.

Maybe there'd been a reason Cade had told no one. Had he hoped something would turn up so his impetuous proposal would become moot?

Did he expect Sam to sweep in and take her and Caleb off with him? She was sure his wife would have something to say to that.

Everything was a mess. Slowly, she crossed the room and eased down on the bed. Too distraught for tears, she gazed dried-eyed off into the darkness, wondering what was the best thing to do.

She and Caleb couldn't stay, not now. Knowing Cade didn't really love her, didn't really want to marry her, awkward didn't begin to describe how she felt.

They'd have to return to Florida. The sooner the better. Before any further plans were made or any further action taken for a wedding that would never take place.

In the morning. They'd leave in the morning.

Sometime later, Cade knocked softly on her door. Jordan

didn't move. Even if he opened the door, he'd see the room was dark and assume she was asleep. After a moment, she heard him move away.

Goodbye, she silently called after him. *Goodbye, my love.*

Jordan slept fitfully during the night. When dawn lightened the sky, she rose, and went to shower and change. Sleeping in her clothes had been uncomfortable, but she'd hardly noticed.

Once dressed in fresh clothes, she quietly set about packing. She'd done this before, only this time there'd be no man standing in the doorway asking her to stay.

She almost cringed, remembering how happy she'd been when he'd asked her to marry him.

Why hadn't she realized at the time it was the third choice? He'd first offered her a job, then a chance at schooling. She still didn't understand why he felt he had to marry her, but she wished she'd gone with her instincts at the time that, as a proposal, it had fallen a little short of perfection.

She'd noticed when buying the rings. But she'd wanted it too much to pay attention to obvious signs. Just as she had five years ago when Aunt Maggie warned her to be careful. She was too trusting and too impetuous. Maybe this time she'd learn that lesson.

Her car was parked in the back. When she heard Caleb moving around, she went to get him dressed and then sent him down to see about breakfast. Rosita loved pampering him. Let him have one last meal before they departed. Once he scampered down the stairs, she quickly packed his things.

She wrote a brief note and left it in the study, where Cade

would see it. She assured him she would repay the cost of the surgery and thanked him for all he'd done for them both.

Taking both suitcases to the car, she put them in the trunk, fairly certain no one had seen her.

She joined Caleb for breakfast, complimenting Rosita on her cooking, and thanking her for all she'd done for them.

"My pleasure. If things don't go the way you want, you must tell me. A woman takes more interest in how her own house is run than a man, I think. You'll be in charge. I do hope you will keep me on."

Jordan nodded, knowing there would never be a change. Even if Rosita didn't run things perfectly, Jordan wouldn't be here to notice.

"You run this home, Rosita. Nothing will ever change that," Jordan said, knowing how true it was.

After breakfast, Jordan took Caleb outside.

"We need to have a talk, Caleb. And we need to drive in our car," she said.

"Okay."

Jordan had to get his car seat from Cade's sedan, and she almost held her breath lest someone see her and ask what she was doing, but the ranch was quiet. The cowboys were out on the range, and Cade and Penny were in the office on the other side of the house. Amelia rarely came over to the big house until closer to lunchtime.

Jordan would miss her. She regretted not being able to tell her goodbye. But she dare not risk it. She'd write and make sure Caleb sent a picture or something.

As they drove down the driveway, Jordan did all she could

to keep her feelings numb. Turning her back on the man she loved was the hardest thing she had ever done. But she couldn't live where love didn't bloom.

By the time they stopped for the night, Jordan's stoicism had broken. Once a cranky, confused and unhappy Caleb was asleep, she took a shower and cried until the water ran cold. Slipping into her nightshirt, she climbed into bed, falling asleep almost as soon as her head hit the pillow.

She hated leaving, but hated the thought of living with Cade when he didn't love her even more. Had he been bailing her out as he obviously was used to doing with his cousin? She refused to be a burden.

The next morning, she felt groggy and cranky herself. Her eyes were swollen from her crying and her energy level flagging. But her determination never wavered.

She pushed on eastward, despite Caleb's demands to return to the ranch. She tried over and over to explain to him they had to return home, but he was inconsolable. He wanted to see Cade, to see Amelia, to play with the dogs and pet the horses. To learn to ride and get his own pony. And learn to become a cowboy.

Through Louisiana, Mississippi and Alabama she drove, trying to ignore her son's tearful pleas, and the demands of her own heart.

Maybe she should have stayed. Even half a loaf was better than nothing, wasn't it? Even if Cade didn't love her, she loved him. Would that have been enough?

Another night of tears and Jordan was ready to do anything to get Caleb to stop urging her to do what she wanted to do more than anything. Finally, she bribed him. If he'd stop talking about the ranch and the people who lived there and stopped pressuring her to return, she'd get him a puppy when they reached home.

It worked like a charm. Too bad she couldn't find the same solace in the thought of a new family member.

Then, as if programmed to add to her frustration and unhappiness, the car broke down just after reaching the Florida state line. Another day waiting for a part, and Jordan was ready to tear her hair out. All she wanted was the sanctuary of her home.

On the sixth day, they reached South Beach. Jordan was exhausted. An afternoon thundershower forced them to close the windows. Since the car didn't have working air-conditioning, she was growing hotter and damp with perspiration and humidity. The drive had been a strain. She wanted a shower, and a quick dinner, then bed. Tomorrow was soon enough to sort through things and make plans.

Tears threatened again when she thought of plans she'd made with Cade. But she resolutely put that behind her.

She'd call Julie first thing. Her friend would help. And once she was back at work, engulfed in normal routine things, she'd quickly forget about Cade Everett and the promise he'd once held.

She pulled into her designated parking place and stopped. Once again, they'd have to get out in the rain. She still didn't have an umbrella. No matter. This time, they could change once they got inside.

She'd get the bags later. Right now, she just wanted the

sanctuary of their apartment.

When she and Caleb quickly rounded the side of the building to reach the front door without becoming totally soaked, he suddenly pulled away, running ahead of her, splashing through puddles, yelling.

"It's Cade. He's come to get us."

Jordan stopped, staring. The rain poured down, wetting her shirt, her hair, her bare legs beneath her shorts. But she couldn't move.

It was Cade.

He rose from the top step and reached down to swing Caleb up and hug him.

"Howdy, partner. You doing okay?" he asked, his eyes immediately moving to find Jordan.

She slowly walked forward. What in the world was he doing here? Her heart pounded. She felt light-headed. Cade, here.

She wanted to run into his arms and have him hold her forever.

But caution prevailed. She'd made her decision. Nothing had changed.

"We missed you, Cade. But Mommy's getting me a puppy, one that can come in the house. Can he come to your house? I want him to sleep on my bed with me, but she said no, he had to stay on the floor. But he can come inside, can't he?"

Caleb was talking almost as much as Amelia did.

Cade said, "We'll see."

He leaned over to put Caleb down, his eyes capturing Jordan's as he walked toward her.

"What are you doing here?" she asked, afraid to believe her eyes.

"First things first," he said, pulling her into his arms and kissing her hard.

She didn't know whether to feel chastised or cherished when he ended the kiss. She knew she felt totally bemused with the rain pouring down, the thunder rumbling in the distance, and her heart racing.

"Did you have car trouble?" he asked.

"Of course," she said with a sigh.

"I've been here two days. I thought I gave you enough time to get home if you didn't have car trouble, but I thought you had to have been held up by something. I worry about you in that car."

"We're fine. Why are you here?"

"Why wouldn't I be? You're here."

"I left you a note."

"Don't you think I deserve more than a brief note? We're getting married, Jordan. Surely you can do better than that."

The rain bounced off the pavement. The scent of wet asphalt filled her senses.

"We're getting wet," she said, wishing he was right—that they were still getting married. She watched him warily.

"So invite me inside."

It was the least she could do. Hadn't he taken her in when she knocked on his door in the rain? It wasn't quite déjà vu. He wasn't sick. She hoped he didn't plan to stay beyond the time it'd take her to explain. She hoped she could do so without making a total idiot of herself blubbering about love and devotion and obligations and all.

As soon as they entered her apartment, she knew it had been a mistake. Cade seemed to take up all the space. She glanced around. The place was neat, if a bit musty, being closed up for so long. But it was nothing to compare with the lavish Everett ranch home.

"Go change into dry clothes," she instructed Caleb.

He ran into his room. She just hoped he'd pick out something that was suitable, and not a bathing suit with a sweater.

Turning, she brushed back her dripping hair.

"You should go change, too," Cade suggested.

"I'm fine."

"You'll get chilled if you stay wet. I'm not going anywhere."

It almost sounded ominous.

"What about you?" she said, stalling.

"I doubt you have anything here that will fit me. I'll be fine. Time enough to change when I return to the motel."

She brought him a towel and then went to her room to put on dry clothes. She was nervous, no denying that. Why had Cade come? She thought she'd explained everything in her note.

He looked so good. She wanted to fling herself into his arms and let him hold her. But she couldn't do that again. She must never forget that.

Reasonably dry, she returned to the living room. Cade had taken off his shirt and hung it in the doorway to the kitchen. It was too damp to dry quickly, but he was probably warmer with it off.

She definitely was, unable to stop staring at his broad chest.

He held out a rumpled sheet of paper. It was her note.

She looked at him.

"I thought it explained everything."

"Now that you know who Caleb's father is, are you hoping for some kind of reconciliation?" he asked.

Jordan was dumbfounded.

"Of course not."

How could he ever imagine such a thing? Hadn't she told him more than a hundred times over the last week she was in Texas how much she loved him?

And hadn't he been silent every time? She should have listened to that.

"Then you changed your mind about getting married."

She nodded.

"Why?"

"I said in the note."

"That it would be better for us to go our separate ways? Better how?"

"I'm very grateful for what you've done for Caleb," she began, but he interrupted.

"Grateful be damned. I don't want your gratitude. I never did."

"But I don't think you wanted my love either, did you? Wasn't I just an obligation you felt saddled with?"

"No." Cade sounded firm.

"I've had a lot of miles to think through. Do you

remember asking me to marry you?"

"Of course."

"I was third choice."

"What?" he said in disbelief.

"It was third choice. First you offered to send me to college, then find me a job. When I didn't take either of those, you came up with marriage."

"I didn't want you to leave."

"And I don't want to live with and compete with a ghost."

That would end the discussion. He couldn't come back against that.

"What are you talking about?" he asked.

He ran his fingers through his hair and stared at her, a frown marring his features.

"I still don't know why you asked me to marry you, but you don't love me. You love Marissa. You always will. I didn't want to be second best."

He crossed the room in three steps and took her in his arms.

"You are not now nor ever will be second best. Marissa is dead. Yes, I loved her. A part of me will always love her, I expect. Don't you still love your aunt even though she's dead? But I'm not *in* love with a dead woman. I've known that for a while, ever since you came into my life. Didn't you say life moves on? It does. I've been given another chance at the golden ring. Another chance to love a woman who means everything to me, to build a new family, starting with Caleb, but hopefully continuing with more kids of our own. Sadly, Marissa is gone. You're alive, vibrant and enchant me beyond belief. When you left—" he hesitated a long moment, gazing into her eyes. "I knew what it would be like if you never came back. I couldn't deal with it, Jordan. I need you. I want you. You're a part of me."

"You have never once said you loved me," she said simply, almost afraid to believe what he was saying.

The facts spoke for themselves. She'd trusted a man long ago and been let down. She wasn't sure she was up to it again.

He looked away, as if in pain, releasing her arms and crossing his own across his chest. Then he faced her again, his eyes wary.

"Sorry about that. I regret it. I didn't know."

"Know what?"

"I didn't know how much I loved you until you left. It was worse than Marissa's dying. At least her death was an accident. Nothing either of us could prevent. And it was over and done with. But your leaving—suddenly I realized what my life would be like without you in it. No bright-eyed optimism, no wide-eyed wonder, no laughter, no loving. It was a pretty bleak picture, let me tell you. And there wasn't the clean break as with death. You're still alive and so am I. All I could do was plot how to get you back. This time, fate wouldn't win. You and I belong together, Jordan. I love you with a love so strong I can't imagine going on if you don't marry me. If you don't spend the rest of our lives with me, I don't know what to do. I can't live in this world and know you are also in it and not with me. Come back. Give me another chance, and I won't blow it this time. I'll tell you every day how much I love you."

Jordan's heart began a heavy beating. Her hopes rose sky

high. Tentatively, she reached out a hand and rested it on his cool skin.

"You really love me?"

"Oh, darling, yes, I love you. More than anything."

He leaned down and kissed her.

His skin heated, warming her. His muscles bunched and moved as he pulled her closer for a deeper kiss. Her own blood heated, chasing the last of the rain's chill away.

Caleb came into the room and stopped when he saw his mother and Cade kissing. Cade heard him and slowly ended the kiss, looking over at the small boy.

"Why are you kissing Mommy?" Caleb asked.

Cade held out a hand and Caleb came over. Scooping the boy up, Cade held him in one arm, his other firmly around Jordan.

"It's what mommies and daddies do," he said.

"Are you my daddy now?" Caleb asked.

"I'm not your biological father, Caleb," Cade said. "But from now on, as long as you live, I'm your Dad."

Epilogue

It was a mob scene. The fresh graduates streamed out into the crowd, looking for relatives and friends. The hot June sunshine beat down, causing those in the graduation robes to wish the ceremony had been held in December.

Jordan spotted Cade, easy to do when he was the tallest man in that direction. She waved, and he caught her eye, grinning over the crowd. In only moments, he drew near, carrying little Emma. Caleb walked proudly by his side. Amelia trailed behind, letting Cade do the work of making a way through the sea of people. She'd worn a frilly pink organdy dress complete with a broad-brimmed Southern belle hat to the ceremonies.

Cade reached Jordan first.

"Congratulations, Ms. College Graduate."

He kissed her. Emma fussed, and Jordan reached out to take her in her arms and nuzzle her soft cheek. At two, she was a handful and wanted to get down. Jordan felt her slipping.

"No, you don't," Cade said, taking her back. "We'd lose you in this crowd. You stay with Daddy."

Caleb hugged his mom.

"I want to go to college and graduate when I get big," he said.

At nine, he was almost as tall as his mother. Compared to Emma, he seemed so grown up.

Jordan kissed his cheek. "And so you shall."

"Goodness, what a crowd," Amelia said, pushing through and hugging Jordan. "Are you feeling all right? I declare in this heat all I want to do is have a cool lemonade and sit in the shade. You weren't the only pregnant graduate. Did you see those other two? I thought that gal with the dark hair might deliver on the stage she's so huge."

Jordan smiled and nodded, resting her hands on the swell of her stomach. Their next child was due in two weeks. She'd known it was cutting it close, and was grateful she had the chance to take part in the graduation ceremonies. It'd been a long time coming. She wished her Aunt Maggie knew.

"Are you ready to head for home?" Cade asked, his arm around her shoulders, steering her away from the heart of the crowd.

Home. The Everett ranch, where she and Cade had returned for their August first wedding five years ago. It would always be a magical place to live—because Cade was there.

He'd adopted Caleb shortly after their marriage, explaining to the young boy that his biological father was Cade's cousin, which that made him and Cade related by blood, so now Cade was making it legal. He'd always be Caleb's dad.

As he was to Emma, their precious baby girl born two years ago. And to the baby she was now carrying.

Cade refused to invite Sammy to family events since discovering his part in Jordan's life. Sammy had given Cade's name in Florida when on spring break to thumb his nose at his cousin and make sure no one could discover he'd skipped out when he was supposed to be in Texas. He'd gotten a kick out of playing the big honcho like his cousin. Only he'd never be the man Cade Everett was.

Few others in the family knew all the ins and outs, but those that did had welcomed Jordan and Caleb with open arms. The others had no reason to hold back. She had the family she so longed for.

As they settled in the big sedan, Amelia insisted she sit in back with Caleb and Emma. Cade glanced at his wife when they pulled away and crawled through the heavy traffic.

"I for one, am glad you won't be making the trip to Dallas anymore. I worried every day you did."

She patted his arm and smiled serenely. "I know, but I was careful every time. History won't repeat itself."

She knew he still worried about other drivers, fearing something would happen to his second family as it had to his first. Jordan did all she could to allay those fears. Only time would completely heal his fears.

And she hoped for another fifty or sixty years at least.

It was amazing, actually, that he loved her so much. In the five years they'd lived together, her own love had grown, as had Cade's. She never suspected when knocking on the door in the rain so long ago that life would turn out so happy. Back then, all she'd wanted was the operation for Caleb's eyes.

Now, she had more happiness than she could ever have

hoped for. She had long ago forgiven Sammy. Because of him, she'd found her true love.

He looked at her, meeting her eyes, the knowing reflected in his.

"I can't wait to get you alone," he murmured for her ears alone.

"I'll love that," she replied, her smile as bright as the Texas sunshine.

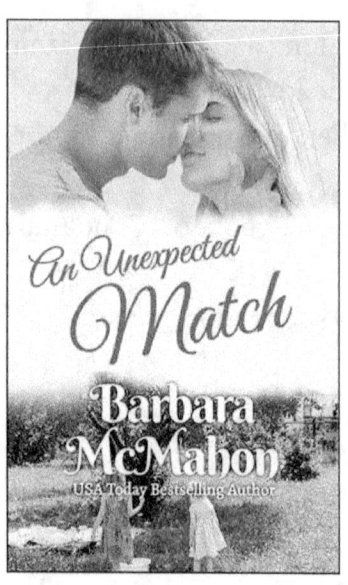

Did you enjoy this story?
If so, you may enjoy AN UNEXPECTED MATCH,
Book Two in the Making a Family Series.

For a complete list of Barbara's books, visit her website at:
www.barbaramcmahon.com/books.

If you liked TEXAS TEMPTATION book,
please consider leaving a review.